Incredulity

by Kathy Zebert

© 2015 Kathy Zebert. All rights reserved.
www.kathyzebert.com

Editor: Lauren Tweedy
Cover Design: Kathy Zebert, Lauren Tweedy
Author Photo: Melody Hood, Innamorata Photography

Publisher: Words in Color Publishing
wordsincolorpublishing@gmail.com

ISBN: 978-0-9967848-0-1

Library of Congress Control Number: 2015915584

1. Romance 2. Legal Thrillers

Printed in the U.S.A.

The inspiration for this book comes from my love of many things: my faith, my family, my friends, my profession, and cowboys.

For my children, Ali and Lauren, my greatest accomplishments in life.

For my brother, Criss Zebert, my A team.

For my best friend, Pam Martin, who agrees with me even when I'm wrong.

And for my colleagues, the court reporters, captioners and CART providers all over the world, who spend countless hours listening to, caring about, and taking down the words of other people's stories.

Acknowledgments:

Alan, Jerri, Angie, Mona B., Mona D., Donna, Janet, Karen and Tamara

Table of Contents

Prologue 1
Chapter 1: Hello, Darlin' 5
Chapter 2: Serendipity 16
Chapter 3: Roped and Tied 27
Chapter 4: Vertigo 71
Chapter 5: Game Face On! 85
Chapter 6: Manna From Heaven 90
Chapter 7: The Silent Heroine 115
Chapter 8: Trailblazing 142

INCREDULITY
Prologue

It was going to be a beautiful Monday in court, notwithstanding the 20-page docket on Callie's calendar. Over the 15 years she'd been a court reporter in Travis County District Court, the criminal calendar had grown by nearly 50 percent, and docket call days had become extremely mundane and depressing. But today would be different. "Bring on the criminals. Nothing will bring me down today," she said to herself.

Callie had just returned from the most romantic and relaxing four days she'd experienced in a very long time. Although she'd been doing a great job of keeping her new love interest a secret from her coworkers for the last several months, it was becoming exceedingly difficult to hide the curious warm glow she was sporting. Callie was normally upbeat and congenial, even when she didn't feel the part. If she was ever in an unhappy place in her mind, those unhappy thoughts never made it to her eyes or her smile. But there would be no need to pretend today; her mood was more genuine than ever.

As she finished her final lap in the pool for the morning and grabbed a towel to begin drying herself off, the memories of her time with Dominic over the last four days swept over her again. *Wow! Is this really happening? I don't want this to end,*

Kathy Zebert

she thought.

    Showered, dressed and out the door in her normal time of 30 minutes, Callie stopped for coffee for herself and Judge Hamilton. She'd be with him all week, and she knew he loved chocolate-glazed coffee from Java Joe's. As she entered the courtroom, Callie set the judge's coffee on his bench and began to power up her equipment and make sure her real-time connection to the judge's computer was running smoothly. Ah, success! Ready for docket call, with time to spare, she sat quietly while sipping her coffee and thinking of Dom.

    On the bailiff's cue, "All rise," Judge Hamilton took the bench and gave Callie a great big smile when he saw his favorite coffee on the bench. "Good morning, Ladies and Gentlemen. Let's get started with this lengthy docket," Judge Hamilton began. "The first case on the docket is the State of Texas versus Jose Rodriguez." Case after case began to be announced, and the morning was going fast.

    It was nearly noon, and there were two more cases to be called. Callie hadn't made eye contact with any of the defendants, as was her normal course. She was strategically situated in the courtroom so that she could hear well, and after this many years, she rarely even looked up as the cases were called. She simply wrote the words she heard, allowing her to remain emotionally unattached to the defendants.

Incredulity

On the next case called, however, that practice would come to a screeching halt.

"We're here in the matter of the State of Texas versus Dominic Jaxson, with a charge of Murder in the first degree."

"Jonas Spence, on behalf of Mr. Jaxson, Your Honor."

"Good morning, Mr. Spence."

"Good morning, Your Honor. We'll waive the formal reading of the indictment."

"All right, sir. Mr. Jaxson, how do you plead?"

Wait...what? Callie had been writing without thinking all morning, and it took a few minutes for the words to sink in. She looked up to see if what she'd heard was real. As she reluctantly glanced over to the defendant's table, she felt sick. *Oh, my God! Oh, my God! Oh, my God!* That was all she could think to herself. Her heart began to race, her neck became hot, and with each beat of her pulse, she felt as if she were playing out a scene in Hitchcock's Vertigo.

No! No! No! This isn't happening! Not my Dom. Callie was beginning to spin out of control, and the words she continued to write became blurry. She couldn't bear to meet his eyes. It was just too much. As Callie heard Dom's deep and raspy voice answer, "Not Guilty, Your Honor," she fought off the tears. The range of emotions swelled inside her. *Please, God, let this be a dream, and wake me up!* As Dom left the courtroom, Callie kept

Kathy Zebert

her eyes to the floor, and the last case was called. Judge Hamilton announced the lunch recess, and Callie ran to the bathroom and threw up her morning coffee.

What the hell am I going to do? she thought, sitting lifeless in her office chair and wiping the tears from her eyes. *I can't sit on this case, but I also don't want to be associated with any murder. There's not enough Calgon in the world to take me away from this. But wait a minute. Dom couldn't have committed murder, could he? I could never love anyone who could be guilty of murder.*

Callie began to think back over everything she knew about Dom, dissecting every minute she had with him from the first day they met. Did she miss some clue?

Incredulity

Chapter 1: Hello, Darlin'

As Callie began to shut down her laptop and steno machine at the end of a very long Monday in court, she felt the need to unwind and get away from the gruesome and stressful words that filled her head. Where could she go for fun without listening to anyone talk or running into people she knew? *Oh, I know,* she thought. *I've been wanting to try Shenanigans to listen to some jazz, and it's just far enough away that I won't run into anyone I know.*

Although Callie worked in Austin, she lived in Dripping Springs, a small suburb nearby, and Shenanigans was a new little hotspot located on Lake Travis, just a 15-minute drive away. Getting out of the house wasn't the norm, as Callie didn't have much of a social life. In fact, she hadn't dated in several years. She'd been pretty much married to her job since her husband passed away and her two children moved out. But the need to be around adults who weren't associated with the judicial system was just what the doctor ordered for the day. Great music and a glass of wine, with the gentle breeze blowing off the lake, was going to provide Callie that much-needed relaxation.

The trip over on 2222 with the BMW's top down had done a number on Callie's long blonde curls, but it was too beautiful a day to resist. Besides, the feeling of hugging the curves without

Kathy Zebert

hitting the brakes outweighed any silly worry about mussing up her hair. It brought back memories of her youth, on those special occasions when Callie's dad gave her the keys to the Mercedes to pick up something from the store. Of course, she took the long way for thrills on "Jumpers Hill." Navigating tight curves and sudden bumps in the road were what made this Southern woman's heart race.

As she pulled into the parking lot of Shenanigans, her mood was immediately uplifted. What a beautiful little oasis this was, with its palm trees and exotic feel on the outside. A quick check in the visor mirror and a few twirls of the curls with her fingers and she was good to go for the evening. Callie didn't know it, but in just a few short minutes, her life was about to get much more interesting, in ways she could never imagine.

Callie saw an open spot at the bar and ordered her favorite late-harvest Pinot grigio wine. Staying consistent with her need to unwind without hearing words, she headed upstairs to the top deck of the three decks surrounding the back side of Shenanigans. *This is the place where heaven meets the earth,* she thought as she found the perfect table for two facing the lake. *Awesome,* she thought. *One chair for me, and one for my purse.*

In Callie's nights on the town in her 20s, she called this extra chair beside her "the attractive man chair." Back then, she'd kept her purse in the chair beside her as an indication to others that she was waiting for someone. And she was... for the next unknown but gorgeous man she wanted to sit next to her. But these days, it really didn't matter what they looked like. She was perfectly content on her own – well, with her purse, which didn't say a word.

There wasn't a cloud in the sky, and Lake Travis was as calm as she'd ever seen it. The two made magic as they blended together to form the horizon. Life was good. The band hadn't started yet, and it was just after 6:00 p.m. This gave Callie the perfect opportunity to sit quietly with her thoughts, her purse, and her wine. About four sips into her Pinot, she realized that the stress was beginning to melt away. It was at this point that she found herself wishing her husband Mike was sitting beside her. He would have loved this view of the water.

It had been a tough six years, after losing Mike to cancer. Coupled with losing her dad last year, the grief was almost too enormous to bear. These two men had been giants in Callie's life, and she believed they were the source of her strength. What pulled her through, however, was her faith in God, her belief that she'd see Mike and her dad again, the love she had for her family, and her career. As a court reporter, Callie was doing important work. She was safeguarding the record of the crimes against the people of the state of Texas. Her work made her proud, and it was something she took very seriously. It was her footprint in the sand, as it were.

As Callie's thoughts wandered back and forth between times gone by and today, she smiled. Over the course of her life, she had been blessed beyond measure by an abundance of love, and a heart big enough to overcome the pain that comes from the loss of that kind of love. It certainly hadn't been easy to go it alone, but still, she smiled. Who could frown while enjoying this breathtaking view?

Deep in thought, Callie hadn't realized that the top deck had begun to fill up quickly. She finished her first glass of Pinot and motioned for the waiter. "Excuse me. Could I have a glass of water and another glass of late-harvest Pinot, please?" Water between glasses of wine would be in order if Callie was going to stay to listen to the band. No DUIs for this court reporter. There was too much to lose.

The waiter went off to retrieve Callie's order, and Callie went back to her thoughts. Just as she began to block out the noise while returning her focus on the horizon, a raspy, but strong male voice said, "Pardon me, ma'am." Callie, saying nothing, reached inside her purse for some cash to pay for her drink and looked up to find someone other than her waiter.

There he stood: a vision of gorgeousness in a Stetson cowboy hat, starched white button-down, a pair of Levi's and Justin ropers. Callie knew the difference between a drugstore

Incredulity

cowboy and the real thing after this many years in Austin, and this was definitely not the drugstore variety.

"Yes?" Callie said with a smile.

"The deck seems to be full, and I came to watch the sunset. Would you mind if I watch it from here?"

Now, what was that about Callie wanting peace and quiet? That went right out the window when the aroma of his Acqua di Gio cologne consumed her senses.

"Of course," she said, as she moved her purse from the chair to the table in one swift motion. "I'm Callie."

"Dominic, ma'am. It's a pleasure. Thank you for sharing the seat. It's been a long day."

"For me as well," said Callie.

As Dominic sat down, he removed his hat, because all real cowboys knew to do that when they sat next to a lady. Callie had met lots of cowboys since her move from Mississippi to Texas, and one of the things she noticed was that many of them used the cowboy hat to cover the fact that they were balding. This wasn't the case with Dominic, however. As the hat came off, Dominic's stark blue eyes really stood out next to his jet-black hair. Callie was mesmerized, but didn't want to stare. Besides, both of them were there to view the sunset. So as the waiter brought her water and wine and a Corona for Dominic, they sat in silence and enjoyed the beauty before them.

Kathy Zebert

Sitting in silence with a stranger would normally be awkward, but nothing about this encounter could be termed awkward. It was almost immediately comfortable, but not the boring comfortable, like an old shoe. It was the kind of comfort you feel from trying something new for the first time and being in sync with it, like throwing your first bowling ball and scoring a strike. The sunset in that moment seemed to be binding them together, as if it were a gravitational force that neither of them felt the need to control.

As the sun said its final good-bye and drifted below the horizon, Callie looked over at Dominic and said, "Absolutely gorgeous, wasn't it?"

"Yes, it is," he replied, his eyes already on Callie. "Oh, you mean the sunset? Yes, but it couldn't hold a candle to that smile of yours," Dominic said, as he winked, grabbed his hat and got up from the chair. "Thank you again for sharing the sunset with me. I'll let you get back to your evening, Callie."

There was no way Callie could let this handsome stranger walk in and out so quickly. Even though it was out of character for her, she asked, "What's your hurry, Cowboy?"

Dominic hesitated for a moment and said, "Oh, I thought you might be waiting for somebody. You had your purse in your chair. I just didn't want to interrupt the rest of your evening."

Callie couldn't help but laugh out loud, because, after all,

Incredulity

that was the intent of the purse being there. "Oh, no," she said. "It was just a handy place for it to be, and it helps me ward off evildoers."

"Well, then, if you're sure you're okay with the company, I can't think of anywhere I'd rather be at the moment," Dominic said as he planted his hat and sat back down.

Over the next few hours, they decided to order dinner and began to get to know each other, talking about their past relationships, family, work; the usual topics of conversation after a chance meeting. Although Callie had come to Shenanigans for the purpose of avoiding words, she found herself wanting to hear more and more of Dominic's story. There was so much more to this man than she had originally thought when her eyes first met his.

Other than their chosen professions, Callie and Dominic had much in common. They'd both lost spouses, they were both in their late 40's, had raised their children, and each had lost a parent. While Callie had grown up in Mississippi, Dominic was born and bred in "Longhorn Country." He'd worked his family's ranch while attaining his bachelor's degree from the University of Texas.

"Have you been in Austin your entire life, Dominic?" Callie asked.

"No. I left after college. I needed to explore the world in

my own way. I found a job in Alexandria, Virginia, and I lived there until about six months ago, when my dad was killed in a car accident. My family needed me here, so I moved back to take over the ranching business."

"Oh, I'm so sorry for your loss, Dominic. I know how hard it is to lose a parent. Even though we know that life comes full circle, we see our parents as monuments, standing still forever, right?"

"Right," Dominic said as he nodded. "So what brought you to Texas, Callie?" Dominic asked. Callie had been so interested in listening to Dominic's story that she really hadn't shared much of her own.

"Well, I guess we're not so different. I was ready to spread my wings too. I grew up in a small city in Mississippi, where my dad was a well-known judge, and I felt the need to be something other than the judge's daughter. I wanted to be close enough to visit, but far enough away to make my own way," Callie responded. "I married soon after that and had my children. And just after my daughter was born, I began my court reporting career."

Dominic must have been as swept away as Callie was, because as the waiter appeared and asked if either of them needed another drink, they both looked up and the tables on the deck were completely empty. It was a Wednesday, and it was nearly

Incredulity

10:00.

"Wow! I didn't realize it had gotten so late," Callie said, as she remembered she had to be at work at 9:00 a.m. "I've got an early trial in the morning. I've got to get home and prepare for it."

Dominic quickly grabbed the check the server had laid on the table between them. "Let me get this." Callie responded with, "Oh, no. I'll take care of it," to which Dominic rebuffed, "Please, Callie. My mom would be really upset with me if I let you pay. Consider it my thanks for letting me sit in on your sunset." How could one mom disagree with another mom who had apparently raised such a gentleman? "Okay, but only because I wouldn't want your mom to be upset with you," Callie said with a smile.

The check was taken care of, and Dominic walked Callie to her car. "This has been just about the best sunset I've ever seen," Dominic said, extending his hand. "Do you think we might do it again?"

Callie was always leery about giving out her number to strangers. A woman alone, especially one in her position, had to be very careful about sharing private information. Although Dominic had been a complete gentleman and Callie felt very safe around him, she decided to be cautious, and said, "Well, the sun sets every day. So it's possible we'll see another one together soon." The response seemed to satisfy Dominic, and he opened the car door for her to get in.

"Drive safely," Dominic said and turned to walk away. Callie pretended to be putting her seat belt on and checking for cell phone messages, but she was really just watching as he walked toward his black F-150 crew cab. *Of course,* Callie thought. *He's a cowboy.*

During the 15-minute drive home, Callie's mind began to spin out of control. The evening had taken an unusual, but wonderful, twist. She couldn't help thinking about the possibility of seeing this beautiful man again and getting to know him better. "Why didn't I give him my number?" she said out loud with regret. "I may never see him again." But those negative thoughts were very quickly dispelled by her confidence in fate. *What a wonderful surprise the night turned out to be,* Callie thought. *If I never see Dominic again, I have a beautiful memory. But boy, am I glad I didn't have another glass of wine tonight.* Callie was experienced enough to know that she shared too much of everything when a third glass of wine was combined with Aqua di Gio.

It was nearly 11:00 when Callie got showered and into bed. She would ordinarily be exhausted by this time, especially after a full day of court, but her brain wasn't ready to sleep. She got up, went to the kitchen and poured herself another glass of wine and retreated to the patio to wait for the alcohol to kick in. *This is*

Incredulity

silly, she thought, as she rolled her eyes and smirked at her 14-year-old behavior. *Why am I letting a man I spent a few hours with take up so much space in my brain?* The answer was obvious. Without realizing it, Callie had missed the exhilaration of anticipating something, someone, new in her life.

The combination of the wine, the breeze blowing off the trees in the backyard, and the moonlight shining on the pool finally overtook Callie's brain, and she headed for bed. In the morning light, however, the thoughts of Dominic came rushing in again, as if only minutes had gone by. She grinned as she said, "Ha ha! I never thought I'd say this, but work is going to be a welcome distraction today. It's normally just the opposite." Callie spent tons of time talking to herself, because... well, she lived alone. She was fine with that; comfortable with the life she had created for herself. Or was she?

Kathy Zebert

Chapter 2: Serendipity

After a very full week of court, it was finally Friday, and it couldn't have come soon enough. Although fleeting thoughts of Dominic had come streaming through to the surface during the week, Callie's focus had to be on the child pornography trial that had taken up the last four days. Not only was it a difficult subject matter, but both the defense attorney and prosecutor were talking at lightning speed, arguing with each other and interrupting witnesses the entire week.

Despite several polite requests from Callie and more stern admonishments from Judge Hamilton to slow down and calm down, it just wasn't in their nature. The jury verdict was a unanimous "guilty" at 6:00 p.m. Callie felt the need to race home and take a shower to get rid of the disgusting stench, after which she was going back to Shenanigans to watch that beautiful sunset and wash away the week with yet another glass of wine. Of course, it certainly wouldn't hurt if she happened to see the handsome cowboy again.

Smiling as she entered Shenanigans, Callie ordered her favorite wine and headed up the stairs to that sweet spot on the top deck. As she reached the top of the stairs and looked to the table, there sat Dominic, looking out on the water. Wow! I can't believe he's here. It appeared that fate was on her side today.

Incredulity

As Callie approached the table, she said, "Excuse me, sir. Is this seat taken? I see no purse in it." Dominic couldn't hold back a gorgeous smile and said, "I don't need a purse. I'm pretty sure I could hold my own if anybody tried to sit in the spot I was saving for you."

"Aww! What a sweet thing to say! I was really hoping to run into you tonight, but I wasn't sure it was going to happen. This is really serendipitous!"

"Well, I've been saving the seat for you every night since the first night we met," Dominic responded. "I make my own serendipity, Darlin'."

Without having sipped the first taste of wine, Callie felt intoxicated and needed to sit before her knees gave way. First of all, the fact that this man had wanted to see her again so badly that he'd been there every night since they met was hard to believe, but overwhelmingly gratifying. Secondly, he'd used the magic word, "darlin'." Callie had fallen in love with that sweet word when she'd first moved to Austin more than two decades ago. "Darling" was an old-fashioned way of referring to someone dear, but "darlin'," without the "G," made her feel safe, as if someone said, "Everything's going to be just fine." It was definitely a verbal bear hug. Dominic didn't know it yet, but he was well on his way to entering the space in her heart that very few people had ever seen.

Kathy Zebert

As Callie sat down, Dominic noticed she seemed a little lightheaded and asked, "Are you okay, Callie?" Callie, not wanting to confess to her weakness just yet, replied, "Oh, yeah. My heel just got caught in a crack in the deck. Good thing the chair was free." She smiled to reassure him. "So how was your week, Dominic?"

Dominic shared the course of his week at the ranch with Callie, but added, "By the way, Callie, you can call me Dom. I think we're way past the formalities, don't you?" Callie nodded in agreement as she took her first sip of wine. Just as before, the conversation became quiet as the sunset did its magical disappearing act over the horizon. Today was different, though. Clearly, the level of electricity was increasing between the two.

"How many head of cattle do you have, Dom?"

"As of today, we have 1,000. I just acquired 200 more head. I'll be headed off to Nuevo Laredo to make the arrangements for transport on Monday morning."

"Is yours just a cattle ranch, or do you have horses?" Callie continued.

"Oh, yeah. I have two quarter horses for breeding, a stable of workhorses and a few that I board for others. As a part of the ranch enterprise, I also offer riding lessons for special-needs children."

"What a wonderful service! Isn't that called equine-assisted therapy?"

"I'm impressed, Callie. How did you know that?"

"I just guessed," Callie said with a giggle, followed up with a quick flip of her hair. "Seriously, I had a court case where someone stole a horse that was being used for that purpose."

"I guess you get to hear lots of interesting things in court, don't you?"

Callie hesitated for a second. "Interesting is the best word I can think of at the moment. In criminal court, I listen to the negative events in people's lives. There are many horrific things I hear that I never wanted to know about, but people are depending on me to make a record of those horrific things."

With a solemn and understanding nod, Dominic said, "That's a huge responsibility. Do those people know how lucky they are to have someone as caring as you are willing to take on that task?"

"Aside from Judge Hamilton, I'm not even sure anyone else is aware I'm sitting there most of the time," replied Callie. "But it's the nature of the beast, I suppose. I'm supposed to remain quiet and unobtrusive in the process; that is, unless the lawyers get out of control. Sometimes I have to speak up, which usually shocks everyone."

Callie wanted to veer the subject off of her job, so she changed the subject and asked, "Are you hungry, Cowboy?"

Kathy Zebert

"I'm so hungry, I could eat a—"

"You weren't going to say 'horse,' were you?" Callie said as she smiled.

"I guess it's not appropriate for a rancher, is it? How about octopus? Nobody rides one of those, do they?"

The couple laughed in agreement and decided to order dinner. Not only was the view amazing at Shenanigans, but the food was the best on Lake Travis, and Callie thought if they left this particular spot, the magical spell would be broken. She wasn't risking that at this moment. Callie ordered a steak salad, and Dom ordered his favorite, chicken-fried steak, with all the trimmings. This was definitely a man after a Southern Belle's heart. Dom didn't know it, but Callie had perfected the art of chicken-fried steak. If he kept saying "darlin'," there might even be a piece of her special pecan-peach cobbler in his future.

The hours went by quickly, but it was Friday night, and there was no worry about an early morning, so Callie and Dom continued getting to know each other until last call. This time, Callie insisted on getting the tab, saying, "My mom would be really upset if I let a cowboy pay the tab twice without having him over for at least one meal."

Dom looked like he sort of suspected that she was making that one up, but he let her take care of the tab. As he walked Callie to her car, he said, "I really enjoyed our second sunset. At some point, do you think we could watch the sunrise?"

Callie was caught off guard by Dom's question and struggled for words, which was a rare occurrence for her. "Well," she said as she checked her cell phone, "According to my weather app, the sunrise will be in about four hours. We could meet at Hilltop Park on Mount Bonnell. Do you know the spot?"

"I know it well," Dom answered. "You bring your gorgeous smile, and I'll bring breakfast. And you can skip the heels."

"Perfect! And don't worry, Dom. The heels are like vampires; they only come out at night."

All of a sudden, without missing a beat, Dom wrapped his long, muscular arms around Callie's waist and planted the most amazingly sweet kiss on her lips and said, "I've been wanting to do that all night."

Callie whispered in Dom's ear, "What took you so long?"

As they each pulled away from the embrace, Dom opened the car door for Callie and said, "I'll see you at 6:00 a.m., at the bottom of the steps. Drive safely."

"You too," Callie said, as she watched him walk away and then pulled off. There wasn't going to be much time for sleep. A quick trip home, a shower and change of clothes and the drive over to Mount Bonnell was going to take up what was left of the time until sunrise. Callie was used to pulling all-nighters when producing daily copy and expedited transcripts for trials, but there were usually several pots of coffee involved. The adrenaline rush created by this new adventure, however, was creating its own jolt of energy. "What a great kisser!" she thought. "I'm in trouble."

Normally, this would be the time Callie would stop, catch her breath and give herself a good, stiff talking to. Callie hadn't always had a level head, but because of her profession and all that she'd seen, coupled with her long-term marriage, practicality and conservative behavior were a part of the woman she'd become. She had worked extremely hard to get where she was, and there was too much to lose by being irresponsible. For some strange reason, though, throwing caution to the wind was winning this particular game of mental tug-of-war.

Feeling rejuvenated from a quick shower, Callie threw on her favorite pair of jeans and a tank top and grabbed her running shoes out of the trunk of the car. "Gorgeous Cowboy – I mean, sunrise – ready or not, here I come!" As she pulled into the overlook parking lot, it was still dark, of course, but the lot was well-lit and easy to navigate. She saw a beam of light coming from about a hundred feet away. As she walked a little closer, there stood Dom, with a Coleman lantern in one hand, coffee and Danish in the other, and two portable chairs strapped onto his shoulder.

"Hey, stranger," Dom said, as he leaned down for a kiss on

Incredulity

the cheek. "I brought more than breakfast."

"You thought of everything, Dom. What can I carry?"

"A cowboy always comes prepared. If you'll take the coffee, I can take your hand."

"Done," Callie said, as she took Dom's unusually soft hand in hers. She wondered how it was that a rancher could have such soft hands, but chalked it up to great genes and cornhusker's lotion and followed Dom up the very steep stairs to the top.

There was something mystical about being at one of the highest points in Austin, alone with a cowboy and a lantern, waiting for the sun to rise. This was definitely one for the book of memories for Callie. Dom placed the chairs in the perfect spot to watch the sunrise, while Callie got the coffee and Danish out. As they sat next to each other and each took a sip of coffee, Dom looked over and gave Callie a welcoming wink. In this peaceful moment, everything in the universe seemed to be in perfect harmony.

The sun crept up from behind the hills very slowly. Of course, the sun rises every day, but today the colors were spectacular. Orange and yellow hues blended together perfectly with an array of blues and purples as the backdrop. The moon was almost completely invisible after a few minutes because of the sun's intensity. Callie and Dom were seemingly hypnotized at this point. It was almost as if God had created this glorious sunrise just for the two of them. They sat in complete silence as they watched, exactly as they'd done with the setting of the sun.

By 6:30, the sun was well above the distant Austin skyline. The Danish and coffee were gone, and Callie was beginning to feel the energy drain from her body. It had been a blissful, but long 24 hours without sleep. The day could have been over at this point, because Callie didn't think a moment like this could be topped. She would soon learn that this was just the beginning of the surprises Dom had in store for her.

"Well," Dom said, "I don't know about you, but I could use some sleep, and I've got to get ready for my trip to Nuevo Laredo on Monday. Are you ready to make our way down?"

"Yes. I've got a weekend of transcripts to work on; after a long and relaxing nap, that is."

As Callie and Dom said their good-byes in the parking lot, Callie reached over and kissed Dom, gently caressing the back of his neck. She looked up at him and said, "Well, we've seen both the sunset and the sunrise. What else is left?"

Dom responded, "Plenty, Darlin'. The wheels are already turning for our next adventure. Are you up for it?"

"If it involves a sweet-smelling, sexy cowboy, I'm on board."

"I should be back in town on Thursday. Have I passed the test to get your digits?"

Incredulity

"Digits?" Callie asked with an inquisitive look.

"Oh, sorry. I mean your cell phone number. Too many ranch hands from Generation Y, I guess. They've got me using their lingo instead of mine," Dom followed with a laugh.

"I knew that, from some of the gang cases in court, but it sounded sort of foreign coming from a cowboy," Callie said. "At first, I thought you were talking about my fingers. Ha ha! If you got past the first kiss, you're on cue for my digits."

Callie and Dom exchanged numbers, a warm embrace and a more passionate kiss than before. They were still alone in the parking lot. This one would have to last several days. As Callie pulled off, she felt completely at peace, although her pulse was still racing from that passionate embrace. She hadn't felt this way in a very long time, and she wasn't sure she should trust it. It would be a good thing to have the next few days as a cooling-off period.

As she got into the house, changed into her lounging shorts and T-shirt and got into bed, her cell phone rang. It was Dom.

"Hello?"

"Hey, Sweet Lady, I was just about to hit the hay for a few hours, but I wanted to make sure you made it home safely."

"Aww... how thoughtful. It was really sweet of you to check on me, Dom. I'm golden, and I'm about to be down for the count. You get some rest and travel safely next week. Give me a shout

Kathy Zebert

when you get back?"

"Count on it, Darlin'."

"Okay. Talk soon."

"Hey, Callie..."

"Yes?"

"The sun won't rise and set the same without you."

As they said good-bye, Callie drifted off to sleep with a sweet smile on her lips. Thinking about anything other than Dom for the next few days was going to be a challenge.

Chapter 3: Roped and Tied

The weekend flew by, and the 400-page trial transcript was under her belt, but not without yet more coffee and 20 hours of work. Ah, the life of a court reporter. *Thank God for my fast 'digits,'* Callie thought, as she grinned a little, thinking of her conversation with Dom. She was really looking forward to seeing him again, but the time apart was going to be a good thing. She needed to remember to think with her head and not her emotions or hormones. She couldn't afford to jump off a cliff without at least looking over the edge and evaluating the height.

After a short Monday in court, with no rush on transcripts for the day, Callie decided to grab a light lunch on the way home, take her laptop poolside and see what she could dig up on her new cowboy via her best friend, Google. Over her career as a court reporter, she'd learned all the tricks to researching whatever she needed to know about, be it spellings, addresses, curriculum vitae of expert witnesses, or case citations. She was a researching rock star!

"Okay, Google. Dominic J-A-X-S-O-N." No more going to the library to research newspapers on microfiche. Callie loved being able to research in her bikini by the pool with a cold beer in hand.

As Callie started perusing through and clicking on links,

she found the usual LinkedIn profile, along with Facebook and Twitter; rancher, UT graduate, a few photos at the livestock shows, an article about one of Dom's quarter horses named Gentleman Jax. The research seemed to be syncing up with his story so far, but as she got further in, she noticed there was nothing past about six months ago. Hmm... maybe he was just a private person prior to coming to the ranch.

"That's enough for now. I think I'll get some more laps in the pool and take a short nap," Callie said. "Then maybe I'll look a little more in depth, perhaps even pay for a background check." A single woman couldn't be too careful, especially with all the technological advances in the 21st century. Technology was wonderful when it was used to improve society, but Callie had seen criminal after criminal come into the courtroom on charges of computer crimes.

It was a longer nap than Callie had intended, and it ended when she awoke to the sound of her doorbell. She wasn't expecting any company, but quickly threw on her shorts, pulled her hair into a pony tail and looked out the front window to see a florist delivery van.

Opening the door, Callie said, "Hey, how are you?"

"Doing well. How are you?" said the delivery man, who was holding the most beautiful orange and yellow roses nestled inside a gorgeous white porcelain vase.

Incredulity

"I must be doing all right," Callie responded, as she took the flowers. "How gorgeous! I've never seen roses this color. What are they called?"

"These are called Tequila Sunrise roses. They're special order. You must be a pretty special lady," he responded with a smile.

"If I'm not, I'm going to try to be now," Callie replied, laughing.

Callie quickly looked for a card and found it hidden inside the stems of the 13 roses. As she touched the envelope, she felt something hard inside. Carefully opening it and peeking inside, she saw a silver filigree key attached to a long, silver necklace. She laid the necklace on the coffee table in front of her and turned her attention to the card, which read...

"The key to the sunrise is in your eyes... D."

Callie was stunned. Who was this man? What was happening? She hadn't gotten roses in a very long time. Her husband, Mike, had sent them to her on special occasions, but he was a pretty practical person, and roses weren't on the list of practicality. These were so beautiful, though! She couldn't stop looking at them, and they smelled like they had just been picked and brought to her front door.

And what about this necklace? "I should probably return it," Callie said to herself. "But I don't want to hurt his feelings.

He obviously went to a lot of trouble to do something this wonderful for me." Dom wouldn't be back until Thursday, so Callie decided to just enjoy the roses and make a decision about the necklace later. For now, she was going to bask in the attention she was getting.

After a nice candlelight dinner with her Tequila Sunrise roses and nice shot of Patron to celebrate her newfound romance, Callie sat by the pool to enjoy the peace and quiet of the moonlit summer night. She couldn't help but think of Dom and wonder whether he was watching the moon at the same time. She couldn't wait to talk to him again to thank him for the sweet thought and gifts, but she didn't want to bother him while he was working. So after a few hours of daydreaming, she headed for bed. She had a three-day trial with Judge Hamilton starting the next day, and rest was on the agenda.

Up early and off to court, Callie could feel her thoughts drifting to Dom and his gifts. "I can't afford to be distracted by that today," Callie reminded herself. "I really need to keep my head on straight for impaneling the jury." It was always so difficult because the attorneys would stand between the jurors and Callie during voir dire, and she had to keep adjusting her chair to see them. No matter how many times she'd asked them to stand still, they just couldn't seem to do it.

The jury was picked and the trial began just after lunch,

Incredulity

with the first few witnesses on and off the stand by the end of the day. The trial was going along fine, and Callie was feeling pretty good about staying focused on the words as they streamed through her brain to her fingers and onto the real-time screen for the judge. It was a good and productive day, and on the drive home, she stopped to grab a burger. Cooking wasn't on the menu tonight. It would be an early night for her in order to get a good start on day two of the trial.

As Callie pulled into the driveway, she noticed a FedEx package sitting under the front porch swing. "Hmm... really? Well, it might be the external hard drive I ordered last week." She pulled into the garage, got out of her suit and into jeans and reached outside for the package. As she looked at the label, she didn't recognize the address and realized it wasn't the package she'd been expecting.

The package felt sort of heavy, and Callie opened it to reveal a gift-wrapped box inside. She quickly ripped off the paper, as she was way too excited to fool with unwrapping it delicately. What she found was a large red leather box with the letter "C" branded into the center, surrounded by a lariat that trailed off to the side. As she attempted to open the box, she noticed that there was a small lock on the front.

Hmm... where's the key? Callie thought. As soon as the word came into her mind, she remembered the filigree key she'd gotten the day before. She went to the top drawer of the dresser where she'd put it for safekeeping and retrieved it. It would be a little crazy if it fit, but to her surprise, it did!

Inside the box was a rolled-up piece of paper with a pretty red ribbon tied around it, nestled within a white satin pillow. As she removed the ribbon and unrolled the paper, she found what appeared to be a piece of a hand-drawn map to something. At the top of the map were the words, "X marks the spot of our next adventure... D." Along the outer edge were instructions on how to get from point A to point B, but Callie hadn't a clue where point A was. She began to chuckle. Another day, another mysterious gift from her handsome cowboy.

"This is craziness!" Callie said out loud. "Things like this don't happen to me." Callie hadn't ever experienced romantic gestures of this kind, and she was a little reluctant to believe it was real. Her mom had always told her that if things seemed too good to be true, they probably were. "I'm not going to let myself get carried away by this man," Callie said emphatically, which was easy enough to say while she wasn't in Dom's presence. She rolled the map back up and placed it, along with the necklace, into the box and placed the box on her desk. It was time to get back to reality and crank out about a hundred pages of an appeal transcript.

Working had become something she did on a regular basis.

Incredulity

A day without a transcript or court was a little jarring, because it happened so infrequently. There hadn't been anything else in her life to focus on, with so many changes having taken place. It had been the only way she'd been able to keep her mind off the sadness she'd felt. These last few days, though, really caused her to focus her attention less on work and more on this new romance. Struggle as she might, the work had to be done.

Night turned into morning, and it was going to be a long day in court. The jury would be getting their instructions, closing arguments would be made by both counsel, and then it was going to be a waiting game for the verdict. After all these years in court, Callie could just about predict how long a jury would be out. Even though this had been a short case, there was a ton of forensic evidence for the jury to get through, and the case wasn't open and shut.

Lunch came and went, and the jury was given the case for deliberations at 2:00. Callie headed back to her office to work and wait, and to try to avoid being distracted by thoughts of Dominic. At about 8:00, word came from the courtroom officer that the jury had a verdict. After a quick few minutes to take down the verdict, she could finally head home. Dinner was going to be skipped tonight for an hour of floating in the pool, followed by a glass of Pinot, a shower, and then bed. Callie was physically and mentally exhausted.

Kathy Zebert

It was around 9:00 by the time Callie got home...to yet another package sitting on the front porch. This package was even bigger than the last. What?! Three days in a row of packages? *Okay. Now, this was too much,* Callie thought. But after her long day, she really needed to smile. The package was from the same address as the one yesterday, so she knew it was from Dom. She wasn't expecting what was inside, though.

"What do you have for me today, my handsome cowboy?" Callie asked out loud. She quickly opened the box to reveal a pair of the most beautiful red leather boots she'd ever laid her eyes on. They matched the red leather box from yesterday, all the way down to her initial/lariat insignia. "Am I going to have my own brand?" Callie said, smiling and deciding to try them on.

As she took the boots out of the box, a card fell out. Inside the card was a pretty red lace hair scrunchie, and the card read, "For a beautiful woman, from head to toe." Callie began to tear up. She had no idea what she'd done to deserve all of this, but she was overwhelmed by the attention, and she couldn't wait to see Dom again. Thank goodness he was coming back the next day so she could thank him in person.

The leather on the boots was so soft, and although they'd need to be worn in, they fit perfectly, to her surprise. How did he do that? This was a man who knew how to get a woman's attention *and* how to keep it. Despite all of Callie's efforts to keep

Incredulity

her guard up, she was failing miserably.

She began thinking about the last few days and remembering what her mother had told her, but then she was reminded of something her sweet dad had said. "A woman who's given gifts should trust that the gifts were given with a kind heart and accept those gifts with a grateful heart." Callie's daddy was just about the wisest man she knew, and she was going to take his advice, relax and just let things happen. She had a good feeling about her cowboy. Why spoil it? "Enjoy the moments," she said to herself.

It was time to get in the pool and have that glass of wine, followed by an enormous amount of daydreaming about Dom, but first, to get out of her clothes and into her swimsuit. Callie was about to return the boots to their box when she noticed another envelope stuck to the side of the box. She opened the envelope, and it was an invitation, with tissue paper and calligraphy. Callie couldn't help but think it might be a mistake, but as she read the invitation, she realized it was specifically for her.

"Mr. Dominic Jaxson requests the pleasure of the company of the beautiful Callie Fletcher at 8:00 p.m. on Thursday, May 25, 2015, at 525 Sunrise Trail, Spicewood, Texas. Upon entry, follow the map provided previously. Leather and lace attire requested."

Kathy Zebert

Callie was so excited just thinking about seeing Dom again. Three days had seemed like three weeks, but he'd made sure that she was constantly thinking about him while he was gone. Tomorrow couldn't come soon enough, but the pool was waiting, and the glass of wine was calling her name.

The sun rose on a beautiful Austin summer morning, after a good night's sleep for Callie. She was beaming as she began to think about what Dom might have in store for tonight. She was anxious to get the day going and finished so that she could see him again. "Bring it, motion hearings! You won't beat me today. I'm going to write like the wind, because I've got a date with a cowboy!"

The day seemed to fly by, and Callie made a beeline for the parking lot. She couldn't get home fast enough to get ready for her date tonight. The time seemed to drag the moment she walked in the door, though. As always, she organized the amount of time it would take her to get ready and get to this mysterious location. Of course, she could have used the time to Google the address to take a sneak peek, but she quickly nixed that idea because it would spoil the surprise. Instead, she decided to read over the directions again, along with the sweet notes Dom had sent over the last few days.

It was about a 45-minute drive, according to the GPS, but Callie wanted to allow a little extra time for unknown GPS snafus

Incredulity

along the way and grab a cup of coffee. As she headed over to Spicewood on 620, she took the time to notice the beauty of the path along the way. Callie loved Austin in the summertime. There was just so much to offer. With work taking over her life, it had been some time since she'd taken a few minutes to just enjoy the beauty that surrounded her.

As she pulled up to the address in Spicewood, she had to take a second to be sure she was at the right place. Wow! What an entrance! Two stone pillars were connected by a black wrought-iron gate, with a Longhorn design in the center, and the name "Silver Spurs Ranch" hung overhead. She checked the address, and it was right, so she eased the car up and the gate automatically opened. Hmm… what is this place? There was no house visible from the road.

After she got inside the gate, Callie stopped to look at the instructions on her hand-drawn map again. She followed each step exactly, parking her car in the spot indicated on the map and getting out to walk. It was a good thing it was still daylight. She walked 55 steps, turned left at the oak tree, walked 30 more paces and took a right at the large boulder, walked across the wooden bridge over a little stream, and when she took the final few steps into a grove of maple trees and looked up, there stood Dominic. He was even more gorgeous than she remembered. Then again, maybe it was just all the attention she'd gotten over the last few days that made him seem that way. Regardless, Callie was excited to see him and gave him a big smile and an even bigger hug.

"How are you!?" asked Callie, as she gave him a kiss on the cheek.

"At the moment, I'm speechless," said Dom. "You look absolutely gorgeous."

"Thanks, Cowboy. You'll do to ride the river with as well." Callie had heard that line in an old Western she used to watch with her dad, and it seemed like the perfect opportunity to use it.

"Well, maybe we should put that on our list of adventures to check off," said Dom, laughing. "But for now, why don't you take a seat. I'm sure it's been a long week, and I want you to relax."

Callie had been so caught up in seeing Dom that she hadn't even noticed anything else. In the middle of the maple grove was a small wooden table, two chairs, candles, a chilled bottle of her favorite wine, bread, assorted cheeses and, her very favorite, Lammes chocolate-covered strawberries.

Thinking that this was quite the spread, Callie took a deep breath and sat down. As she did, she noticed the view in an opening of the trees. What a beautiful little lake! She then realized that she was facing the sun as it began to set. Dom had just created their own personal sunset.

As Dom poured Callie a glass of wine, she said, "Dom, I

Incredulity

have to tell you, I'm feeling completely swept off my feet here, with all the gifts over the last few days and all of this tonight. It's a little overwhelming."

"Why would it be overwhelming, Callie?"

"Because no one has ever gone to this much trouble for me before. I mean, Mike was very kind, and we had a very loving marriage, but this kind of romance wasn't part of our relationship."

"Truthfully, Callie, although my wife, Sara, and I had a great relationship, this kind of romance wasn't something she was interested in. When I tried to do anything like this for her, she thought it wasn't real. I guess the 'cowboy' image in her mind was something different. I just decided to be who she wanted instead of who I was."

Callie thought for a second and said, "You know, if this is you, I'll take more, please."

"Be careful what you wish for, Darlin'," Dom said with a wink, and Callie snuggled into her chair to just enjoy what was to come. As the sun set over the lake, Callie and Dom sat in silence, taking in each other and the view. Dom lit the candles, and when he did, the trees lit up with tiny little lights nestled in the branches. No need to worry about creepy crawlers here. *It just couldn't get better than this,* Callie thought.

But she was mistaken. After they'd finished their wine and

the strawberries were a thing of the distant past, Dom suggested they head up to the house for a moonlit swim.

"You have a pool here?" Callie was surprised to hear about a pool on a ranch. She'd always envisioned a ranch to just be a one-story house with horses or cows, but not much of anything extravagant. Yet again, she was mistaken. She was about to be completely awed.

"Sure. Why not? Cowboys don't just swim in rivers," Dom responded with a little laugh.

"I guess I just totally showed my ignorance about the everyday rancher, huh?"

"Well, I'm pretty sure I have a thing or two to learn about court reporters too. Teaching each other is all part of the fun, right?"

Callie agreed with a nod, and Dom walked her to her car for the drive up to the main house, which was about a mile. No wonder she didn't see it from the road. It was too dark to see anything on either side of the drive up, but as they got closer to the house, Callie couldn't believe her eyes. Boy, this was definitely not the ranch she'd pictured. This looked like something out of a movie set created by Hollywood. Who knew this was back here?

The circular drive in front of the house had a portico, where Callie parked and Dom came over to open her door. As

Incredulity

they entered the house, it was immaculately decorated with cream walls and warm-toned fabrics. It had a huge, open floor plan with floor-to-ceiling windows across the back of the house facing the pool and Jacuzzi. Of course, after that, it was no surprise that the kitchen had state-of-the-art everything and the master bath was as big as Texas.

After Dom had given Callie the grand tour, she asked, "Do you live here all by yourself?"

"Yes. It's way too big for just me, but it's a part of the ranch, and it's home. There used to be eight people living here, between my parents and my siblings. We all went off to do other things, and then after Dad died, I came back, and my mom couldn't handle the memories. So she bought a condo in town and comes out to stay with me every now and then."

"It's an amazing home. And although it's big, it feels really cozy here. I felt comfortable as soon as I walked in."

"It makes me happy to hear that," Dom said. "Ready for a swim?"

"Sure, but I don't have a suit with me. Do you have a T-shirt and shorts, maybe?"

"Oh, I can do better than that," Dom said, as he reached over and grabbed a bag on the table. "I might not have the size just right, but I'm pretty good with these things."

Callie reached into the bag and pulled out a swimsuit with

the tags still on. "You don't miss a beat, do you, Cowboy?"

Dom said, "Well, I always have a plan, and I try to back it up with whatever I need to make the plan work. I guess that's the business brain I was born with."

"I am super impressed! And it's just my size. Thank you so much, Dom! I'll get changed."

The moonlight was amazing, and Dom was even more handsome in his swim trunks. There was just enough hair on his chest to be sexy, and Callie was feeling the wine take hold of her senses and sensibilities. Dom must have read her mind when he offered up a cappuccino after the swim. Ahh... warm and inviting, just like this lovely man.

As the two sat on the edge of the pool with their toes in the water and cappuccinos in hand, Callie said, "So how was your trip, Dom? You really haven't talked about your week at all."

"Oh, it was pretty boring stuff, Callie. I got the cattle checked out with the vet, paid to have them transported, and they're waiting to get through all the border checks. I'm sure it was nothing compared to your week."

"Well, truthfully, I'd rather have been checking cattle than listening to testimony about the rape of a young girl. Sometimes boring is a great thing. Do you have to go back anytime soon?"

"I'll have to make another trip to be sure what I paid for is what I'll be getting. That will be midweek, probably, but just for

Incredulity

a few days. What does your schedule look like for tomorrow?"

"I don't have anything going tomorrow. My judge is off, so I'm off. It's nice when he decides to clear the calendar for a day or two."

Without realizing it, the time had been ticking away. Callie didn't want the evening to end, but she knew she had to drive back home, and it was well past midnight. It was at this point that Dom posed the question that caused Callie to pause and stumble back to the days of her youth.

"So does that mean you can stay for breakfast?" Dom asked with a smile.

Why in the world does the answer to this question have to be so difficult? Callie thought. *You'd think a simple yes or no would suffice.* But immediately Callie's brain kicked into high gear with analyzing the consequences of the answer. If she said yes, would Dom think she was easy and all the romance end? Would she see him again? If she said no, would he be upset and move on?

Dumb rabbit hole! Regardless what Callie's answer was, it was her decision, and she would never know the answers to the silly questions she was asking herself. These were questions that only time and Dom could answer, after Callie gave a response. Callie knew the bottom line was that she didn't know Dom very well, but before she got too far down that rabbit hole, Dom noticed her hesitation and immediately followed up with a total bombshell.

"I've got four guest rooms here, Darlin'. Pick one. I just don't want you to drive home this late at night, and it would really make my day if I could start it off by making you breakfast."

Feeling completely at ease, Callie left the silly thoughts behind and responded with, "Okay. But only if we can make breakfast together."

Dom gave Callie a nod and said, "Now, that's a plan I can work with."

Now that that decision had been made, both Callie and Dom seemed to get their second wind, and sleep didn't seem to be a remote possibility. Of course, it could have been the effects of the cappuccino at midnight, but it was more likely the excitement of spending the night together, without the pressures of intimacy at the moment. Callie wasn't ready to take the relationship to that level just yet. She hadn't been intimate with anyone since her husband, and even thinking about it was a huge step for her.

Since sleep didn't seem to be in the cards, they decided to put on a movie and make popcorn. Yes, it was 2 a.m., but Callie was still up for snuggling on the sofa with a good whodunit on the widescreen. Dom had a projector screen that came down from the ceiling, along with the typical surround-sound system. She

Incredulity

had a smaller setup at home, but nothing as spectacular as this one, of course. *Boys and their toys,* she thought.

Callie and Dom snuggled up to watch the movie, and four hours later, Dom woke up to find Callie still in his arms and smiled. He tried to move without waking her so that he could sneak in breakfast without her help, but he didn't know that Callie was a very light sleeper, and the first move brought her eyes wide open.

"Trying to sneak off?" Callie asked.

"Nothing gets by you, does it, Darlin'?" Dom replied, as he winked.

"Not much. I'd love to take a shower, but I don't trust you to wait for me to help with breakfast."

"What if I agree to start the coffee and grab a shower myself, and then we can get started on breakfast? I'm kind of looking forward to seeing what kind of team we make."

"Deal, Cowboy! The last one out of the shower is a rotten egg. Oh, wait... maybe not. I don't want rotten eggs for breakfast. Maybe the last one out of the shower owes the other a beer."

"You're on!" Dom said, as he got a running start to the shower.

"Hey, that's not fair! I don't remember where my shower is!" Callie began to laugh out loud as she tried to remember where the closest shower was. She may be at a disadvantage because of the unfamiliar surroundings, but Dom had no idea how fast Callie could go from shower to fabulous when she had to.

Dom lost the shower challenge, which not only gave Callie an IOU for a free beer, but also an opportunity to at least get a cup of coffee ready for them both and check out the fridge to see what was available for breakfast. It was completely stocked, surprisingly. Dom wasn't kidding when he said he always had whatever he needed to make sure his plans could come to fruition. As a matter of fact, Callie noticed a pair of shorts and a T-shirt already laid out on the bed for her when she ran past to hop in the shower.

As Dom came into the kitchen, Callie greeted him with a cup of coffee and a smile. "Ready to get our breakfast on, Dom?" Callie asked, as she glanced over the kitchen for utensils and pots and pans.

Dom responded, "Yes, ma'am! Let's get this show on the road."

As the two began their dance in the kitchen, it seemed as if they'd done this before. They were working in perfect harmony, very smoothly getting eggs, bacon and French toast ready like a pair of culinary artists on Top Chef. Both of them definitely knew their way around a kitchen. Breakfast was plated up, and as they ate, they planned the day ahead.

Callie had to head home before lunch, but agreed to come

Incredulity

back later in the afternoon for dinner on the grill. What Dom didn't know was that she had her own surprise for him. Callie would be bringing dessert, something she'd perfected over the course of her life. Her desserts had always gotten the most compliments of anything on the table over the years at family events, and she couldn't wait to see what Dom's taste buds thought.

On the drive home, Callie was consumed by the wonderful feeling she had when she thought about Dom. She couldn't explain it, but he was becoming more and more important to her. Although she'd been trying to find something negative about him, nothing was standing out as a red flag. Was she not looking for them? Well, it *had* only been a couple of weeks, she reminded herself, and it was easy for anyone to put their best foot forward for that length of time. She would just wait and see how things played out and try not to let her feelings overpower her good reason.

Back home, Callie grabbed the mini cake pans and all the ingredients necessary to make "The Cake," as it had been lovingly called for years. It was a luscious dark chocolate cake, with blueberry filling and frosted with white chocolate butter cream. She made it as a groom's cake for her son's best friend, Trey, and it was gobbled up, leaving the beautiful wedding cake to stand there in shame. Callie had no idea it would be such a hit, as it was simply a concoction she threw together because the groom said to surprise him with flavors. That was definitely something Callie knew how to do.

She'd already decided what the design would be: a sunset theme, of course! She baked and decorated the cake in record time and went off to the pool to get a few laps in. Staying fit had always been important to Callie, but it was super important now that someone was seeing her not-so-30 body in a swimsuit... and possibly out of the swimsuit, eventually.

The exercise was invigorating, and time was ticking away. After a quick check of e-mail to be sure nothing urgent needed her attention, Callie boxed up the cake and began her trek back to Dom's. She couldn't wait to see him! "OMG! Stop it right now. Calm your cowgirl boots, Missy! You're not 14 anymore." There was Callie, talking to herself again. And herself responded, "Oh, yeah?! You don't have to be 14 to be excited about a man. Being excited about a man is okay at any age."

Callie pulled up to the gate and headed up the long drive to the house. This time, it was still daylight, and she got a better view of the spread along the way. It was absolutely breathtaking, as far as the eye could see. Was this the Ponderosa? She remembered seeing it once when she took a trip with her parents to Nevada.

Callie's dad loved anything with cowboys, including the

Incredulity

Cowboy Channel, and he was always in control of the television. If you wanted to watch something else, you had to go to another room. While Callie wasn't in love with Westerns, she just loved being in the room with her dad. As she began to reminisce, she started thinking about how much she missed him, but then she smiled as she looked up and said out loud, "You'd love this place, Daddy."

Out of the car, she grabbed the cake and knocked on the door. Dom opened the door immediately and said, "Hey, Stranger," offering a sweet kiss on the lips. "What's in the box?"

"It's just dessert."

"Really? You didn't have to do that."

"Oh, but I wanted to. Baking brings me joy, and you've been spoiling me. I wanted to spoil you back just a little."

"Well, I'm man enough to take it, but I sure hope it's chocolate."

Callie simply smiled as she headed off to park it on the kitchen counter for later. Dom had a glass of wine waiting for her there, and they both stepped out to the patio to enjoy each other while the grill was heating up. The more they talked, the fonder they grew of each other. Callie was beginning to open up and talk about her innermost feelings of love and loss, and Dom began to share more of his story as well.

Dom's parents were married for nearly 50 years when his

dad suddenly died. His mom was a very strong woman, even though she was from another era. Callie could tell that Dom had a healthy respect and love for both of his parents, which gave him a good balance. He seemed to know exactly what he wanted in life and went after it. He most definitely knew how to treat a lady, and he was unafraid to show her who he really was.

Callie had faltered a little along the way. Although her parents had been married for a short time, they weren't a great match, and they divorced when Callie was a child. Callie had moved in with her dad when she was a teenager, never really having bonded with her mother. After she'd moved away from Mississippi, she'd found the first man who remotely resembled her dad's characteristics and married him.

Mike was good to her, and for that, she was grateful. After he'd passed away, quickly followed by her dad's passing, Callie's foundation had been shaken. Dom seemed to come along at a time when Callie had begun to be less sad, but simply content with her life. He was quickly showing her that she needed more than mere contentment, however. She needed way more, and she had so much more to give.

The steaks were amazing, and the baked potatoes and vegetable medley were like none she'd ever tasted. Dom was quite the culinary buff – this cowboy was full of surprises. As the sun began to set over Silver Spurs Ranch, Callie thought this would be

Incredulity

the perfect time for Dom's surprise dessert.

She went inside and unboxed the cake, as Dom watched in curiosity. As she revealed what was inside, Dom stared in amazement. "Wow! You did that, Callie? You need your own shop!"

Callie said, "Yeah, and a half a million in funding to open it," with an eye roll. "Cake decorating is much like court reporting. No one understands the amount of work that goes into it, so they never want to pay you what you're worth. But as I said, it brings me joy. Joy, meet Dom. Dom, meet Joy."

Dom, afraid to touch the cake, walked all the way around it so that he could see all the details. This was a round, mini cake for two, with a little left over. On the outside, it looked just like the Austin sunsets they'd enjoyed, with the perfect blending of orange, red and yellow as a backdrop to black silhouettes of a cowboy and his lady, a Longhorn, a black stallion, and a Texas star, with a rope curling around each. As a topper, Callie had designed a pair of red chocolate boots to match the ones Dom had given her, but added silver spurs with his initials on them. This, to her, was a symbol of their connection to each other.

As she looked up at Dom to ask what he thought, she noticed a single tear rolling down his cheek. She said, "I'm so sorry. Does this make you sad?"

"No, Darlin'," Dom replied, as he wiped away the tear. "A

tear falls when I have no words. And I have no words because I'm so moved. No one has ever done anything like this for me before. Do we have to eat it?"

Callie said, "Well, I guess we could stare at it, but it would be a shame to waste chocolate and blueberries."

"Whoa! You said the magic word! I'm not wasting chocolate or blueberries. What kind of idiot would do that? Let's take lots of pictures before we cut into it, though. Although this will be embedded in my memory for a lifetime, I'm going to frame the photos and put them around the house, because it's just that amazing."

Twenty photos later, from Dom's very expensive camera, the cake was finally cut, and the first bite was all it took for Dom to say, "I'm in love." Callie was happy. She was really happy. It had been so long since she'd said that even to herself. This was so huge that she thought this was something she had to express it, so she did.

"I'm so happy. I just needed to say that."

"You had me at chocolate. I just needed to say that," Dom replied, and they both began to laugh.

The evening could be over right that minute and it would be perfection, so Callie decided she'd leave a little early. She needed to rest for a weeklong trial, and she knew Dom had to get ready for his trip. Exercising restraint was becoming more and

Incredulity

more difficult as Callie spent more time with Dom, but she knew she needed to take baby steps.

Sunday came and went way too fast, and court was going to be a bear the following week. Daily copy transcripts had been requested by both sides for the entire trial, which meant no time for anything else except work. Even though Callie had a great scopist and proofreader and both would be working online with her during the trial to get the pages out the door, it was going to be an exhausting process. She'd already made an appointment for a massage at the end of the week because she knew she was going to be tied up in knots from the physical stress.

Judge Goza was the presiding judge for the week, and Callie really liked him because he wouldn't allow anyone to waste time in his courtroom. Too many repetitive questions were followed by "Move on, Counsel," from the bench. If he followed his norm, this weeklong trial could turn into three days.

Everything went smoothly, with no technical issues between Callie and her counterparts, and the first and second days of daily copy were produced by 8:00 p.m., which is what time Callie left the courthouse. There was just enough time at the end of each day to get home, grab a banana and get in bed for the next day. Lunch had been the tuna and crackers snack kits she always kept in her desk.

Everyone else got a decent lunch break while Callie and her

team worked straight through. Rarely did anyone bother to even ask her if she'd eaten. She'd become the silent listener in the room, and as a result, she was overlooked. She'd given up caring about that many years ago, because she knew the value of her place in the process, even if no one else did.

The jury took the case for deliberations on Wednesday, as Callie had hoped, and came back with a verdict of not guilty, shocking the courtroom and even the defendant and his attorney. Callie knew that jury verdicts are unpredictable, even when most people believe a case is a slam dunk. Sometimes a case hinges on whether the jury liked or disliked one of the attorneys. Sometimes it's a heinous crime, and even without enough solid evidence against the defendant, the jury wants to punish whoever is sitting in that chair.

Since Callie had no vested interest in what the verdict was, she quickly shut down her equipment, left the courthouse, grabbed a cup of coffee and headed for the spa. On her way there, it suddenly occurred to her that she hadn't seen nor heard from Dom for the entire three days. Given all of the extra attention and gifts he'd showered her with last week, she went into her usual hyper-analysis mode again. Did she do something wrong? Did he lose his interest because she hadn't slept with him? Did something happen to him?

"Oh, stop it!" Callie said to herself, as she rolled her eyes.

Incredulity

She'd been busy all week; he probably had been too. It was time to head off to the massage and melt the physical and emotional stress away like the ice cube in her coffee. It was a silly worry, and silly worries never amounted to anything productive.

After an hour of massage with Jennifer and 50 laps in the pool at home, Callie was, once again, rejuvenated. She planned on treating herself to a wonderful dinner, plated on her special china, complete with cloth napkins and candlelight, poolside. She did this for herself every now and then, to remind herself that she was special. After Mike died and the kids moved out, Callie had used the time to treat herself as she'd always treated her family and friends. After all, she deserved some of her own special attention.

After dinner, Callie put on one of her favorite movies, Pure Country. She loved looking at and listening to George Strait. There was lots of sexy about that man, and the movie made her feel good. When she'd first moved to Texas, Callie said to herself that if she ever found a cowboy who wrote a song for her, she'd make it her mission to marry him. Of course, that hadn't happened, but a girl could dream.

About 30 minutes into the movie, Callie got a call from Dom. As she saw his name pop up on her caller ID, her heart began to pound.

"Hello," Callie answered in a sweet voice.

Kathy Zebert

"Is this the sexiest cake-decorating court reporter on the planet?"

"Could be, but only if this is the sexiest cowboy chef on the planet."

"I think we might be in luck, then," Dom said with a laugh. "How's your week going, Darlin'?"

"It was crazy busy, but finally settling down, with an off day tomorrow. Are you back in town?"

"I wish I was, but, no. That's the reason I'm calling. I've hit a snag with the cattle, and I've got to renegotiate because nearly half of them had to be quarantined. I won't be able to get back until sometime next week."

"Bummer. I hope you're not losing money on that deal."

"Yeah, me too, but I'm not worried about that. I just really missed you and wanted to be back sooner."

"Aww... I've missed you too. But you do what you need to do. I'll be around next week."

"Okay. I'll give you a call as soon as I get in. I can't wait to see you again."

"Ditto, Cowboy."

As the two hung up, Callie's desire for Dom seemed to intensify. He may be the man with a plan, but she had a few of her own in mind. He wasn't going to out-romance her. The days seemed to fly by, as Callie went about her normal activities, but

Incredulity

the anticipation of seeing Dom and wondering what day that would finally happen started to get the best of her around Tuesday of the following week.

Finally, on Thursday night, Dom was back, and Callie agreed to meet him for dinner at the ranch on Friday. It had been nearly two weeks since she'd seen him, and she couldn't wait to feel his strong arms around her. As she arrived on Friday, she found Dom waiting at the front gate, with the most beautiful horse she'd ever seen. It was the blackest black, with a white mane, tail and white legs and hooves.

Callie got out of her car and hugged Dom as he stood with the reins. After a long and sweet kiss, she said, "Who's this beautiful creature?"

"It's Dom. Remember me? Oh, you were talking about the horse? Ha ha. Her name is Yin Yang. She's been waiting to take you on a ride before dinner. Are you ready to saddle up?"

"Uhh... I've never ridden a horse before. I love looking at them, but they're a little intimidating because of their size."

"Relax, Darlin'. You'll be with me, and I've done this before. I'm not going to let anything happen to you. Let's take a walk with her first, and I'll let the two of you get to know each other. She has a gentle nature, sort of like me. You will have her complete devotion if you offer her sugar."

"Okay. I'm game," said Callie, as they began to walk on

opposite sides of the horse. Callie began to lovingly stroke Yin Yang's silky soft coat, and it was love in the making. At the gate to the front forty, Dom stopped to open the gate and handed Callie two sugar cubes and told her to feed them to her open-handed. Although Callie was nervous about sticking her hand up to this huge mouth, she calmly did as instructed, and it went off without a hitch.

"I think the two of you know each other well enough to saddle up. Are you ready?" Dom asked.

"Let's do this!" Callie responded.

Dom saddled up and pulled Callie up and over in one swift move, as if he'd done it a million times, and he probably had. Callie was so excited. She was actually riding a horse and loving every minute of it. At a smooth, steady pace, Dom was able to show Callie a good part of the ranch, through little streams, big green pastures, and up the hillside to the most captivating view of the Austin skyline she'd ever seen. Amazing!

As usual, her cowboy with a plan had a bench waiting, with a bottle of champagne chilling. As Dom left the saddle and helped Callie down, he tied Yin Yang's reins to a nearby stump to let her graze. They sat down on the bench, and he opened the champagne, pouring a glass for them both.

"I want to make a toast," Dom said. "I come up here sometimes just to get away from it all and revel in the grandeur

Incredulity

of how beautiful life is here. But it has never looked as beautiful as it does in this moment with you, Darlin'. To you, Callie, for showing me the beauty in life I never thought possible."

Callie began to tear up. She was so overwhelmed by the moment that it left her breathless. Avoiding the oncoming sobbing which frequently followed that feeling, she caught her breath and said, "And to you, Dom, for giving me the passion for life I didn't know existed." They sipped champagne as they sat on the bench in a warm embrace, just being still for the next hour.

They headed back to the house, had another delicious dinner, and again came the question from Dom. "Can you stay for breakfast?"

"I'd love to, but I have an early morning appointment. Rain check?"

"Rain or sunshine, always," responded Dom, with a disappointed look on his face.

Callie did have an appointment the following morning, but it was something she could easily have canceled. She knew that she still wasn't ready to take the relationship to the next level, however. In light of that, she decided it would be better just to remove herself from the decision-making process, taking all the stress off the table. Temptation was becoming more and more difficult to resist, especially when there was alcohol involved. Baby steps were her best choice for now.

Kathy Zebert

As she pulled off, she started to regret her decision to leave, because of the look Dom gave her as they kissed good-bye. But then she remembered a conversation she had with her dad about this topic, once she was old enough to talk about these things. Callie had expressed how difficult it was to decide the appropriate time to be intimate in a new relationship, because the outcome of the decision was impossible to know.

In response, he'd said, "It's simple, Baby Girl. The outcome doesn't matter, as long as you're making the decision for yourself. The decision to have sex with someone has nothing to do with them; it is only about you. Whether they leave for other pastures or they stay because they really care about you, you did what you wanted at the time you were ready."

Her decision being confirmed by her thoughts, Callie got home and began to prepare for the week. Sunday came and went, and the days turned into weeks of new surprises and adventures for Callie and her cowboy. There was canoeing on Town Lake, cycling in the Texas Hill Country and a hot-air balloon ride from Austin to San Marcos. Dom knew how to have fun, and Callie was soaking it all up.

As the relationship grew, so did her trust in him. About a month had gone by when Callie finally decided to invite Dom over for dinner. This was her home with Mike, and it was a huge step to invite another man into it, but she was ready. It was her turn

Incredulity

to spoil him. She knew he was out of town again all week, but she sent him a text, asking him over for Saturday dinner.

He responded with a text of, "Love to! Do you need a background check first?"

She followed with, "No. Your first child will do."

"She's pretty rotten, so we have a deal."

"LOL! CU at 7:00 on Saturday?"

"What can I bring?"

"Just UR sexy smile. I'll take care of the rest."

"Can't wait 2CU."

"Ditto, Cowboy!"

On the menu for Saturday was Callie's chicken-fried steak, mashed potatoes with milk gravy, mac-n-cheese and buttermilk biscuits, and a very special dessert of walnut-peach cobbler. She would forego her normal tendency to make large portions, because this meal always put everyone to sleep. All this starch, sugar and fried food was no longer in her usual daily diet, but this was a special occasion, and she really wanted to treat Dom to some Southern comfort food.

It had been a slow week, but Saturday finally came, and the house had been cleaned from top to bottom. Dom had called to let her know he was on his way. By 6:45, dinner was prepped, the wine was at the perfect temperature, the table was set poolside, and Nora Jones was doing her awesome thing on the iPad. Dom rang the doorbell about five minutes later, and as Callie opened the door, there he stood, wearing his unbelievably gorgeous smile, with a guitar case in one hand and some sort of framed art in another.

Greeting him with a hug and kiss, Callie said, "Hey, Stranger! What's all this?"

Dom replied, "You're providing the meal. I thought I'd provide the after-dinner entertainment. I've been working on something special for you."

Callie had grown up playing lots of musical instruments, with the keyboard as her favorite. She had no idea Dom played even one musical instrument, let alone the guitar. He was continuing to reveal surprise after surprise. He was quite the Renaissance man.

Dom set his guitar down on the fireplace hearth, and Callie asked, "How did I not know you played the guitar?"

"I'm just peeling back the layers one at a time, Darlin'," Dom said, as he turned the frame around to reveal the artwork inside.

"Oh, my God! What have you done?!" Callie said, as she put her hands up to her face. Dom had taken one of the photos of the sunset cake she'd made for him and had it blown up, matted and custom fit into an antiqued oak frame.

"I didn't ever want you to forget how special this made me

Incredulity

feel," Dom said.

"You are the most amazingly generous and thoughtful man, Dom! What did I do to deserve all this?"

"You were born," Dom said as he reached over and gave her a kiss.

It was at that very moment that Callie decided she was ready to take that next baby step... well, more of a giant leap. There was nothing holding her back now. Dom had gained her complete and total trust, and she was ready to move forward. The seductress inside was now confident enough to bubble up to the surface and show this man how special she thought he was.

Dinner went off without a hitch, and the small portions were a great decision, given Callie's plan for the rest of the evening. Dom helped her clear the table and went to the fireplace to get the guitar. Callie pulled up the ottoman, front and center, and Dom began to sing...

> Sunset's calling, me and you
> Sunset's calling, just us two
> Words don't cover the beauty of us
> All there is, is sweet and silent dusk
> We make sense in a senseless world
> Sitting in silence as our love is unfurled
> Whether on land or across the sea
> Sunset's bringing you home to me...

Kathy Zebert

The rest was a blur, because at this point, Callie was so overwhelmed that the tears took over all of her senses. George Strait had nothing on this man, and that's something she never thought she'd say. He had such a deep but soft voice, and it was clear that he'd written the song just for her. Dom watched Callie's reaction to his serenade, and it was as if he knew that he had finally lassoed her heart. He'd had to work hard to gain her trust, but it was clear that he felt she was worth every single minute.

Dom finished the song, and Callie, without saying a word, reached in for a passionate kiss, softly took his hand and led him up the stairs to the bedroom. It was no surprise that the two of them were just as compatible in the bedroom as they had been in every other aspect of their lives. He was a very patient, passionate and gentle lover, and Callie was falling hard and fast.

A few hours later, as they lay in each other's arms in complete bliss, Callie realized she'd forgotten to put the cobbler in the oven. "How about a swim while dessert is in the oven?" she asked.

"Didn't we just have dessert? I'm not sure you can top what just happened here."

"That's for sure! Okay. Well, we can just leave the walnut-peach cobbler and vanilla bean ice cream for another time."

Dom quickly gave her a kiss, jumped up, grabbed his

Incredulity

boxers and said, "Last one down to the kitchen owes the other a glass of wine."

Callie said, "You win!" She knew the cobbler had to bake first anyway, and she wanted to freshen up and put on a swimsuit. By the time she got downstairs, Dom had preheated the oven and poured the wine. The swim was energizing, and Dom ate an entire bowl of cobbler and ice cream, much to Callie's delight.

Callie looked at the clock and it was nearly midnight. With eyebrows raised, she said, "Can you stay for breakfast?"

Dom smiled, "I was only waiting for you to ask. But be careful. It might be hard to get me to leave."

"I'm not worried," Callie said, laughing. "I already know you have a business trip Monday."

After dessert had settled, the two made their way back to the bedroom and fell asleep. Callie slept better than she had in a very long time, waking up on Dom's chest. She could hear his heart beating, and looked up to see the cutest little-boy smile on his face.

Almost as if he sensed her watching him, Dom opened his eyes and said, "Mornin', Darlin'. Did you sleep well?"

"The best I've slept in a very long time. You?"

"I second that emotion," he said, as he reached over and gave her a passionate kiss. Round two of their newfound intimacy was even more in sync than round one. After a satisfying morning of lovemaking and a shared shower, they headed downstairs to prepare breakfast together.

Dom was hesitant to leave before noon, but he knew he had to get things ready for his trip. He said he'd be gone for a couple of weeks this time, but he'd call and check in when he had time. As they kissed good-bye this time, Callie's heart sank. She would miss him more this time than she had before. Work was waiting on her desk, though. It was time for a reality check, but not before hanging that beautiful artwork, right on the wall in front of her desk.

Over the next few weeks, Dom became busier than ever with ranch business, but Callie had a three-week trial on her agenda. They were making time for each other, but it was difficult with work getting in the way. New love and court reporting didn't tend to mix very well. Callie knew she had to maintain her focus during proceedings, and it was really hard to do that with Dom drifting in and out of her mind. Of course, that was just inside the courtroom and didn't take into account all of the late nights Callie was required to work to get transcripts completed and delivered.

At the end of September, Callie's trial was over. And although an appeal had been filed, the judge decided to clear his calendar, which meant a four-day break for Callie. Dom's schedule coincidentally cleared at the same time, so they decided

Incredulity

to take advantage of the opportunity and take their first trip together.

Dom had a cabin in Ruidoso, New Mexico, and it would be the perfect place to relax and unwind together. Neither Callie nor Dom had shared their relationship with anyone. They didn't want to risk breaking the magic of the spell they were under, and they knew that outside pressures could sometimes have a negative effect on a new relationship. But more to the point, whatever time they had together, they didn't want to share it with anyone else. Callie's coworkers, friends and family were certainly wondering what this new glow was all about, but she explained it away as just having gotten through her grief and looking forward.

As they arrived at the cabin on Wednesday, Callie found it to be exactly what she'd expected. Although it was in the middle of nowhere, completely surrounded by trees and mountains, it was complete with all the modern amenities, including a Jacuzzi that they would definitely be dipping into. Prior to their arrival, Dom had the caretaker stock the fridge with enough food for the week. The only thing on the agenda was time alone.

Over the next few days, the relationship grew stronger and stronger. Callie knew Dom had something up his sleeve, but, as usual, she didn't have a clue what was coming. He had continued to be a breath of fresh air at every turn. There had been lots of laughter while sharing more stories of their childhood, hopes and dreams about the future, great food and amazing sex.

Friday afternoon, a storm began to brew, and the skies grew dark. As a light rain began to fall, Dom sat down and pulled Callie close to him. He began to tell her how much these last few months had changed his life and how much she meant to him, as she listened intently.

"Do you remember our first horseback ride?" Dom asked.

"Of course, I do. Yin Yang and I became great friends."

"I've been thinking back to that time, and all of the sweet memories we've made before and after that. We are so compatible in ways that I've never felt with another human being. We fit together to create a perfect balance. You are the Yin to my Yang."

"I couldn't agree more, Dom. I honestly can't imagine my life without you in it."

Dom reached into his pocket and brought out a small, red box, with the familiar "C" monogram encased by a lariat.

"Dom, what did you do?"

"I wanted to give you something that symbolizes the way I feel about you. So I had this designed a few weeks ago."

As Dom handed the box to Callie to open, she could feel her pulse racing. Inside was a platinum ring in the shape of a horseshoe. One-half of the horseshoe was covered in black onyx gemstones, and the other half was covered in diamonds. Callie

Incredulity

was beside herself. Dom had shown his generosity on so many occasions, but this was really extravagant and so special.

"I'm speechless, Dom. I love it! It's perfect!"

Dom took the ring out of the box, took Callie's hand and placed the ring on her finger, after which he said, "I love you, Callie, in every way a man could love a woman."

This was the first time that word had been used, and Callie knew the significance of it. "I love you" gets thrown around way too often in this world. Callie had never said those words to anyone she didn't truly love, not even her friends. She knew Dom felt the same way, from their conversations about it in general. If what she was feeling wasn't love, she'd never known the meaning of it.

"I love you too, Dom, more than I ever imagined my heart had the capacity to feel."

Almost immediately after the words came out of Callie's mouth, the rain began to tap on the windows, the thunder roared and the lightning clapped. It was as if the heavens approved of Dom and Callie's proclamation.

"Well, that was interesting. The only thing missing from that was trumpets," Dom said, and they laughed uncontrollably, followed by a consummation of their love in front of the fire.

Saturday morning came way too soon, but Dom had to get back to the ranch early for a meeting on Sunday. Someone wanted to breed with one of his mares, and they were going to need to iron all the details out.

Callie had docket call first thing Monday morning anyway, so she needed a day to get her mind back in court reporter mode. Couldn't they just pretend she was there and let her stay here? They hardly noticed her except when they wanted something read back. What would be the likelihood she'd be missed?

But Callie knew her absence would definitely be noticed, and she and Dom said their reluctant good-byes on Saturday afternoon. They passionately kissed and embraced, planning to see each other on Wednesday.

Chapter 4: Vertigo

When Callie and Dom parted on Saturday, there was no way that either of them could have envisioned the turn of events that followed. Dom had been arrested on Sunday, unbeknownst to Callie, and Callie had no idea what had been waiting for her on this morning's criminal docket. How could she have gone from ecstatic to traumatized in less than 48 hours?

Sitting in her chair in her office, staring at the wall like a deer in headlights, Callie ate a saltine and drank a sip of water to try to calm the nausea. As she recounted every moment she'd spent with Dom, her heart was telling her that there was no way her gentle cowboy could ever have committed murder. But her head was combing through the details of the last 90-or-so days and remembering all the business trips. There was also the fact that her research on Dom early in the relationship had gone cold on anything beyond six months prior to their meeting. And what about the strange term, "digits," he'd used when he asked for her number?

These things by themselves were nothing, but together, were they more than just circumstantial evidence? She'd heard that term thousands of times over the last 15 years of trials, and she knew that A plus B plus C didn't always lead you to D, but she also knew that people don't just get arrested without evidence.

Kathy Zebert

The problem was that she didn't know what the evidence was, because that wasn't discussed at an arraignment.

What was she going to do? She couldn't talk to Dom. She couldn't be associated with this case, because she had a huge conflict of interest. No one knew about her relationship with Dom, and she was so grateful they didn't. If she told someone now, could she be implicated in some way? She would definitely be interviewed. Could she lose her job? Could she lose everything? She reached for the trash can as she felt another wave of nausea coming on.

Just as her eyes rose from the trash can, she noticed movement in front of the closed door just before an envelope slid towards her feet. She nearly lost her balance as she attempted to get up, but took a second to regain her composure and picked it up. Based on what just happened in the courtroom, she was afraid to open it, but she did anyway.

Inside were a handwritten note and a business card: "We should talk. Meet me in the parking lot of Mable's Tavern ASAP. Come alone." As she looked at the business card, she was astounded to see the name and title on it: Frank Kendrick, Special Agent in Charge, Drug Enforcement Administration. Geez, could the day get any worse? What was this about? Although she wasn't sure she wanted to know, she stuck the crackers and bottled water in her purse and headed off to this very

Incredulity

mysterious meeting.

As Callie pulled up to the empty parking lot of the tavern, there was a lone silver sedan backed into a spot in the corner. She began to quiver as she pulled up to the car, not knowing what to expect. The day had already rocked her world like an immeasurable earthquake. She wasn't up for any aftershocks, but the cracks in her foundation were about to get wider.

Callie pulled up to the driver's side of the sedan, and the man inside rolled down his window and motioned for her to do the same. She took a deep breath and exhaled as she hit the window button, and Frank introduced himself and began to explain the purpose of the meeting.

"Hi, Ms. Fletcher. I'm Frank Kendrick, with the DEA. I know you're wondering why you're here and why all the mystery. We have a common interest: Dominic Jaxson."

Callie heard the words and a million questions began to infiltrate her already-clouded mind. Who was this man, and how did he know her? Had she fallen into some dark world she knew nothing about? DEA?! This couldn't be happening.

Frank continued, "Dominic has been working with us on a DEA special assignment as an undercover field operative. Over the last six months, we've been investigating an elite drug task force inside the Austin Police Department, known as Cobra. The details of the investigation are highly classified, as is Dominic's cover. As his handler, I am aware of your involvement with him and his arrest yesterday."

The wheels in Callie's mind began to turn. Frank's explanation wasn't answering any of her questions. Dominic was an undercover operative? Was she merely a part of this cover? Was anything she'd experienced over the last three months real? Just as she was about to ask questions of this complete stranger who seemed to know all about her, he handed her another envelope.

Callie opened the envelope as Frank continued even further in a monotone voice. "This is a gag order from a federal magistrate, Callie. Feel free to read it, but the gist of it is that you're not allowed to discuss your involvement with Dominic with anyone, either inside or outside of your employment with the court. Leaving the case is not an option, because it could lead to Dom's cover being blown. We have no idea whether Dom is guilty, but we are too close to completing this investigation to risk blowing it all now."

Frank finally stopped talking long enough for Callie to try to absorb what he'd just said. There were many questions she could ask, but the one burning question was this: "So you want me to sit in that chair and pretend I have no feelings about this case and no interest in the outcome? This is a huge conflict of interest, and I could lose my license, my job and everything I've

Incredulity

worked for, if anyone finds out."

"It's your choice, Ms. Fletcher. If you violate the judge's order, it's guaranteed that you'll lose all of that, in addition to your freedom," Frank said, at which point he rolled up the window and proceeded to drive off. Callie jumped out of the car and threw up again. She was stuck. There seemed to be no way out of this situation. She couldn't talk to Dom. She couldn't talk to Judge Hamilton or her coworkers, her children, her best friend, no one in the world.

It was at that point that Callie had a light-bulb moment. Oh, yes, she could talk to her best friend, because her best friend, Pam Miller, was a genius lawyer in San Antonio. She definitely needed some legal advice on this issue, and a shoulder to cry on as well. She was not going to let this situation take everything away from her, regardless of what any federal judge said.

Callie was going to protect Callie, first and foremost. She couldn't believe Dom had put her in this situation, but she had to put her emotions about him aside until she came up with a plan. For now, the only thing she knew was that she wasn't going to sit idly by as an observer and wait for the possibility that someone else could run her life into a ditch.

Callie began to feel less nauseous, at least for the moment. She'd need to get back to work for the afternoon docket, but the first stop on the way home was to an out-of-the-way convenience store for a cheap cell phone that couldn't be traced to her. It was a good thing she had cash left over from her trip to New Mexico; she didn't want to risk leaving a paper trail of any of her activities. She had no idea if her calls were being monitored, but given the day's earth-shattering events, she was in hyper-alarmist mode.

Court couldn't end fast enough today. She put aside her drama to get back to work, and numbness was all she could feel for the rest of the day. It was as if she'd had an entire bottle of wine on an empty stomach. She could only hear ringing in her ears, coupled with the words coming at her in the courtroom. She kept her head down and remained completely faceless, as she normally did. Today, she was very happy not to be noticed.

The day went by lightning fast, and Callie quickly got to her car and sped off to the old country store near her home. She knew they sold throwaway cell phones, and she also knew there was no video surveillance in the store. She and the cashier had joked about the fact that the shotgun under the counter was all the protection he needed for the store.

In and out of the store without conversation, Callie quickly got home, poured herself a stiff shot of tequila and sat down by the pool to call Pam. Although she felt the need to shower this awful day away, she really needed to get some advice about how to proceed so that she could protect herself. Pam would know what to do, because she always did, and she always had Callie's

Incredulity

back.

"Hello?" Pam answered with an uncertain voice.

"Hey, Pam. It's Callie."

"Oh, hey, girl! What number are you calling me from? What's wrong? I can tell by your voice something's happened."

"I'm calling from a burner phone. I think I'm in trouble, and I need your help."

Callie's voice began to crack as she recounted her every moment with Dom from the point they met until today's gut-wrenching events. Pam was listening intently in her usually patient way, with an "Oh, my God!" at every unbelievable detail. What a rollercoaster ride this had been for Callie. As she was repeating the details out loud to Pam, she felt every emotion humanly possible.

"What am I going to do? How can I protect myself? How could I have been such an idiot to fall for someone I barely knew?"

Pam responded very calmly, "First things first, my friend. You've done nothing wrong. Secondly, have you heard of the term, 'Innocent until proven guilty?' He's been arrested, but you have no idea what evidence led to that arrest. You have a good head on your shoulders, and your instincts are always right on."

"Now, as for what you should do," Pam continued, "write everything down in a journal, as best you remember it, including dates and times of your interactions with Dominic, as well as your conversation with the DEA agent today. We'll call this an affidavit, of sorts. When you're finished with it, let me know. I can be there in about an hour to collect a dollar as my retainer, at which point you'll be my client. I'll have my assistant meet us, notarize the affidavit and take it back to my office for safekeeping. From this point on, say nothing about this to anyone. You do not want to violate a federal judge's order. Regardless of what happens, I've got your back, both as your lawyer and your friend."

Callie had been holding back the tears for as long as she could possibly manage, but Pam's calming support had allowed the tears to come rushing to the surface, and she began to sob. She could barely speak, but managed to get a thank-you out. Pam was such a gem. She was the sister Callie never had, only without all the drama. They'd been best friends for nearly 20 years, and had been there for each other through every joyous and devastating life circumstance.

"You get some rest, Callie, and try not to worry about this. Go to work tomorrow as if nothing has happened. As a court reporter, you know how to cover your emotions. I'm going to do some checking with my contacts in Travis County and the DOJ in the meantime, to see what I can find out. I'll see you soon."

"I love you, Pam. Thank you for always knowing what to say," Callie said. Hanging up the phone, she put it in the glove box of her car.

Incredulity

The night was going to be long, and Callie was going to have to muster every ounce of courage she had to walk into that courtroom tomorrow. Her first instinct was to run, as it normally was, but when it came to "fight or flight," Callie knew the right choice was to stay and fight. For now, though, she was going to cry out all the tears. She really wanted to talk to Dom. Who was she kidding? She really wanted him to wrap his strong arms around her and make this all disappear.

There wasn't enough alcohol in the house to numb all the emotions at this point, and Callie knew that drinking always exacerbated whatever mood she was in. Opting for hot tea instead, she headed back inside to brew a pot and change into her swimsuit for some laps. Keeping her body busy always seemed to keep her mind from stepping in and ruining things.

Unfortunately, actually making it to the pool without being reminded of Dom was impossible. There was the artwork on the wall, the boots, and the jewelry, all of which were in her periphery, but she could put those things away for now. Getting rid of the memories surrounding them, especially those in the bedroom, was going to be futile. She was going to have to deal with that... somehow.

After 25 laps and three cups of peppermint tea, Callie felt much better. The universe had certainly thrown her a curveball, but she'd been through cancer with her husband and dementia with her dad, and this was nothing compared to those two things. She had no power over illness and death, but she had power over emotional stress. She could simply turn it off. She would turn it off, no matter how impossible it seemed.

Callie's sleep was restless, but morning came in its usual fashion, and it was time to get to work. She smiled as she passed the sheriff's deputies at the security station. Surprisingly, even to her, she smiled her way through the entire day. No one knew about her devastating circumstances, and no one was going to know. During the lunch hour, she'd taken the opportunity to journal, as Pam had instructed, making a copy for herself at the local office supply store. She wanted to get the details down while they were fresh in her mind. After work, she gave Pam a call, and they agreed to meet at a quiet lakeside park just outside Dripping Springs. No one was ever there during the week.

Pam showed up early, as usual, with a much-needed hug for Callie, and introduced her to her assistant, Amanda. The affidavit was signed and notarized, at which point Amanda left to return to the office in San Antonio. Pam had gotten some information from her contacts at the state and federal agencies, but was waiting for Amanda to leave so that she could share what she'd learned.

"Okay," Pam began. "So I've gotten the details of Dom's arrest. The victim was a woman by the name of Angelina

Incredulity

Villarreal. She was a 27-year-old bartender at Boys Will Be Boys over on Guadalupe. Do you know the place?"

"Yeah," Callie replied. "It's a strip joint with the usual associated criminal element. I've never been there, of course, but I hear random cases involving the place on a regular basis."

"Yeah. Well, apparently, Dominic and Angelina were seen on numerous occasions together in the late hours after she got off work. They were seen arguing just a few hours before her body was discovered in a Dumpster a few blocks away. She'd been strangled by some sort of rope, but we'll know more after the autopsy is finished."

"Oh, my God! What in the world was he doing at such a disgusting dive? And what was he doing with this woman? Wait a minute. Do you have the date for all of this? Maybe he wasn't even there. Maybe he was with me, and I can prove it."

Pam pulled out her notes and said, "The arrest report says they were seen arguing on the night of September 15th at about 11:40 p.m., and her body was found in the Dumpster by a homeless woman at about 1:30 a.m., on the 16th."

Callie didn't even have to look through her notes for the answer. She knew that Dom had been on one of his trips on that day, because it was just prior to their trip to Ruidoso. Of course! It wasn't going to be this easy to vindicate Dom and get herself out of this horrific nightmare. As she'd just now realized, the so-called trips must have been another lie.

"I can't believe this is happening!" exclaimed Callie, putting her hands over her face.

"Calm down, Callie," Pam said as she reached for Callie's hand. "Listen to the voice of reason for a minute. This evidence is circumstantial, at best. There could be a very logical explanation for all of this. We just don't know what that is at this point. What we do know is that Dominic was working for the DEA. And I have more information about that from my contact at the feds, so hang on."

Callie moved her hands away from her eyes and took a deep breath and exhaled, saying, "Okay."

"As Frank told you, the DEA has been investigating Cobra. What he didn't tell you is that Dominic was recruited as a special undercover agent because of his expertise in this type of case. Dominic's knowledge of the cattle industry as a business, coupled with his previous training as a field operative by the CIA, made him a prime candidate for this investigation."

"What are you talking about? CIA? How did I not know this?"

"It's the CIA, Callie. You're not supposed to know about it. CIA agents, past, present or future, aren't allowed to divulge their association with the agency, not even with their families. To do so would put lives at risk and defeat the purpose of being a spy."

Incredulity

Callie began to laugh, because, well, Pam was right, but also because crying was no longer an option. This entire situation was ludicrous, and Callie's desire to run was getting stronger by the minute. She wasn't sure she could take any more information. It just kept getting worse.

Pam continued, regardless. "Dominic freelances with the agency on occasion when his expertise is needed, as it was in this DEA investigation. He's been deep undercover for the last six months, investigating Cobra, as you already know. Apparently, the DEA got a hot tip from another investigation that someone inside Cobra was confiscating cocaine, skimming some off the top, and distributing it throughout the country via cattle transport. That's all I know right now. And so it's clear why you and Dominic are where you are at the moment, and why it has to stay that way for a little while longer."

Callie stopped laughing at this point, and the wheels began to turn. She understood now, and her faith in Dom was somewhat restored. She still couldn't wrap her mind around this murder, though. How did that tie in?

And then came a moment of clarity for Callie. Although it seemed that she was stuck in an untenable personal and professional situation, being on the inside of the case gave her an advantage she wouldn't otherwise have. Some of her questions could be answered by looking at the charging documents and listening to testimony. All of a sudden, Callie felt the stress leave her shoulders, and her heart rate began to slow as she took a deep breath. Life had handed her lemons, and she was going to make a cheesecake.

Pam had to get back to San Antonio, but offered a huge hug and said, "Everything's going to work out, Callie. I'm always here if you need me. Just keep your emotions in check, focus on your job, and let the system work."

Callie had never been very good at letting someone else control anything that would affect her life's circumstances, but she reluctantly agreed and said, "I love you, Pam. Thank you for riding this wave with me. I'll keep you posted."

Chapter 5: Game Face On!

When Callie began court reporting school, one of the first things she learned was that facial expressions were a big no-no during proceedings. Over the course of her career, she'd found this was sometimes difficult to pull off. There were those times when she wanted to cry, laugh, roll her eyes or smirk, but she'd always been able to make those faces only in her mind while maintaining an expressionless face. Dominic's trial, however, was going to require Callie to exercise the kind of restraint that only a nun could imagine, but she could do it. She had very little choice under the circumstances.

A few hours after Callie got home from her meeting with Pam, she decided to get on her computer to check her docket for the schedule. She'd been so frazzled at the time Dom's case was called that she hadn't noted when it was set for trial. She knew she'd have to be mentally prepared for the day, so having a date certain in her mind was going to be necessary way ahead of time.

Callie logged into the court's calendar and discovered that the trial was set to begin on Monday, November 13, and was scheduled to be one week. One week to decide the fate of someone's life didn't seem long enough, but the thought hadn't entered Callie's mind before. Not only did it affect the person who was on trial, but all the people who loved them or who had been affected by their actions. The process of a courtroom trial had a much deeper impact than she'd ever imagined.

    The next several weeks were going to be unimaginably painful. Sitting at her kitchen table with a cup of coffee and her head in her hands, the only things she could feel were the steam coming off the top and her heart beating like a drum in her ears. Her body had been physically aching all over, but the numbness had now set in. She began to sob, but then said out loud, "Stop it." She knew the tears would help nothing, and she couldn't afford them at this point. She needed to take control of the situation. She was nobody's victim.

    Almost instantaneously, the tears stopped, as if she'd turned off the kitchen faucet. A swim was in order to clear her head and relax her body, so off she went to let the cool water wash over her for 25 laps. It was just what the doctor ordered. Callie felt much better after an invigorating workout, and decided it was time for a homemade dinner and a plan. Exercise followed by comfort food, although an unusual pairing, was exactly what she needed.

    Grandma's homemade macaroni and cheese fit the bill. Grandma and this favorite dish had worked magic on many of the problems in Callie's life. This particular problem required a second helping, though, with something chocolate for dessert, along with a glass of wine to help her sleep.

Incredulity

Callie put on some soft rock music in the background and sat down to eat. At the end of her cathartic meal, she picked up her bottle of wine and went to put her feet in the pool. The sun had already set, thank goodness. She didn't need that little reminder of Dom at the moment. What she did need was a battle plan; one that would allow her to get through the next several weeks before trial, but more importantly, through the trial.

In the quiet of Callie's backyard, with lights glimmering off the pool water, she looked up at her two favorite stars. She liked to call them Mike and Daddy, because they were the brightest ones in the sky, and seeing them made her feel as if they were watching over her.

Callie was deep in thought when all of a sudden, she felt the weight of a hand on her right shoulder. It startled her, and she immediately turned around. No one was there. *Surely it was just the wind*, she thought, but she realized there was no wind. *It was probably the wine*, Callie surmised as she returned to her thoughts. A few minutes later, she felt the weight on her shoulder again. Although she couldn't explain this anomaly, she didn't need to. The weight of that hand on her shoulder allowed her to take in a deep and calming breath. It was as if Daddy, or Mike, or God, or maybe all three, were saying, "It's going to be okay, Callie."

It was at that moment that clarity arrived. As clearly as

Kathy Zebert

Callie could see those stars in the sky, her plan came into her vision. She was not going to just sit idly by and watch her life happen. She was not in a movie theater with a bucket of popcorn. She was the director and writer of her story, and although she couldn't control the circumstances at the moment, she was going to have control over her role and how things played out for her.

Pam was right. Dom was innocent until proven guilty of this horrible crime. She was also right about the fact that Callie had great judgment about the character of the people she let into her inner circle. This traumatic turn of events had caused her to question that. Pam, and the hand on her shoulder just now, were reminders that she should trust her instincts.

If there was one benefit to being forced to sit and hear this trial, it was that being on the inside gave her access to crucial information she wouldn't otherwise have. Having that information gave Callie the internal strength to move forward. God had brought her this man, and God had a plan for them both. Callie was going to have faith in that and take her faith with her to the battlefield, aka the courtroom.

The weeks leading up to the trial seemed to fly by. For everyone else at the courthouse, it was business as usual. For Callie, it was putting her head into her work and struggling to keep her emotions at bay. She missed Dom so much that it felt as if she was grieving again, but she was not going to let grief

Incredulity

interfere with her resolve. Trial would begin in two weeks, and her game face was on. Bring it!

Chapter 6: Manna From Heaven

The anxiety Callie had been feeling over the chain of events in her personal and professional life had begun to subside over the last few weeks. Time had done its job in healing this wound, at least temporarily. She'd been able to plaster that familiar smile across her face, disguising the gaping hole in her heart and the fear of losing everything. Court reporting had taught her to hide her emotions, which was paramount at this point.

This would be a short week, with Judge Hamilton out of the office at a conference, so Callie was in and out of her office, filing transcripts with the clerk's office and getting more editing finished on appeals that had been stacking up. Deadlines kept her mind occupied. After a quick lunch with a colleague on Tuesday, she returned to her car to go back to work and begin working on a monster appeal. Reaching for the car door, she noticed something white under the wiper blade on the windshield. It was another envelope, reminiscent from weeks before.

Oh, no! Hello, anxiety. Here we go again. Callie didn't want to open the envelope, and she immediately threw it in her purse. No one would ever know she'd gotten it. She would ignore it and it would go away.... except that she couldn't. She went straight back to her office and tried desperately to begin working,

Incredulity

but the distraction was just too much. She rolled her eyes, reached down and retrieved the envelope from her purse, took a deep breath and opened it.

Inside, there was a small key, with a typed note, "UPS Store on Brazos, Box No. 4224. There's more to the story than you know."

The first thought that entered Callie's mind was that the feds were going to help Dom after all. But that was quickly dispelled when it occurred to her that they wouldn't be giving the information to Callie if that were the case. She'd been told to stay quiet. So who was this note from, and what was in the box? Should she take this to the authorities? No way! Undercover meant under cover, and Callie wasn't taking any chances. Besides, she didn't know what was in the box. She did, however, call Pam to tell her what was going on.

Of course, Pam's first comment was, "Stay out of it, Callie. We don't know who this came from or what's at play here." Although Callie agreed with her, her desire to find evidence that could clear Dom and release her from the invisible prison bars surrounding her was overwhelming. So off she went to the UPS store. It just so happened that she used this store often, and it wouldn't appear unusual if someone saw her going in and out.

The UPS store was just a few blocks away, so it was an easy walk for Callie. She quickly headed for the mailboxes and opened the box to find a manila envelope. She pulled a tissue out of her purse and grabbed the envelope, carefully sliding it into the outside pocket of her purse. She wasn't leaving any trace of her fingerprints, just in case she needed to turn it over to someone. She decided to head over to a small, quiet coffee shop for a quick look at the contents of the envelope.

With a caramel latte in hand, she sat down in a corner booth and opened the envelope with another tissue, sliding out the documents inside. The first piece of paper exhibited copies of receipts for drinks from Boys Will Be Boys, a strip club on the outskirts of town. The name on all the receipts was the same: Brandon Brett. The dates on the receipts ran from the beginning of July to August 14th.

Callie knew Brandon, but only because he'd testified as an investigator on multiple occasions, and she'd seen him at a number of county social functions. He was one of those good-looking, but arrogant police personnel she'd run across every now and then. Every time he testified, she rolled her eyes internally, thinking, *He thinks he's above the rest of us.* He was an intelligent man and a decorated officer, but he reminded her of a cocky athlete she'd known in high school, also named Brandon.

The next page in the series of documents appeared to be some sort of purchase order receipt for several hundred feet of rope of some kind from the local farm supply in Austin. It was

Incredulity

purchased by the Travis County procurement office, but similar to the first document, Callie had no idea what the importance of this document was or why it was included.

Callie turned the page, and the last piece of paper was another typewritten note. "Read the indictment and the narrative of the arrest report carefully." Clearly, this information was offered from someone on the inside of this case. Who could it be? And why were they contacting her about this? If there was evidence of some kind in Dom's case, why not just go to the police?

There were too many questions and not enough answers, but Callie thought it was best to keep quiet and look over the court documents. There was nothing to lose by looking at them. Her plan all along was to read over everything the weekend before the trial, simply because she wanted to be mentally prepared.

Whatever these documents meant and whoever they came from, it was obvious that someone thought they were important, and this just moved up Callie's timeline for reviewing the case materials. For now, she was heading back to the courthouse to work. She was going to need time to think about what she'd just read, look through everything and decide what, if anything, she was going to do about any ambiguities she uncovered when comparing these new documents with what was already on file.

With 250 pages edited, Callie looked up at the clock on the

wall of her office, and it was 4:55. The end of the day was here, and those documents were burning a hole in her purse. She couldn't wait to get home and begin her research. Of course, she knew what she was doing was unethical, but she didn't find this information on her own and she was only looking into it, and she hadn't put herself in this position; she was merely praying for a way out of it.

Callie sat down after dinner, wine in hand, and began to log into the court's back-end system. She pulled up the arrest report, and the first thing she noticed was the investigating officer's name: Brandon Brett. She now had a connection with at least the first document. The date of the incident was on or about August 14th, 2014, at or around 12:30 a.m., and upon an initial skim of the narrative, Boys Will Be Boys popped out at her.

Ding, ding, ding! The date of the last receipt for drinks by Brandon Brett was the date of the incident on the report. This was certainly no coincidence. From talking to Pam, Callie already knew that the victim was a 27-year-old woman by the name of Angelina Villarreal, a bartender at Boys Will Be Boys, and that Dominic was reported to have been seen arguing with the woman on the night before her body was discovered. Even though the details were painful to read, she was grateful that she was reading them now instead of hearing them for the first time at trial. At least this way, she'd have time to absorb some of the shock.

    Investigator Brett's narrative indicated that the body of Ms. Villarreal was discovered inside a Dumpster in an alleyway located behind Sugar Loaf Bread Company, which was just a few blocks away from Boys Will Be Boys. Her body was discovered by a homeless woman who was scavenging for bread scraps from the bakery.

    The chief medical examiner, upon autopsy, determined that the cause of death was asphyxiation, and the time of death was approximately 2:45 a.m. A search of the scene discovered a lasso in a storm drain about 50 feet away from the Dumpster. Forensics had been able to match the hair found on the rope with the victim's hair and the pattern markings of the rope were identical to the pattern marks on the victim's neck.

    As Callie flipped the page, the narrative continued, it seemed, to build even more evidence against Dom. During a search of Dominic's ranch, Investigator Brett reported that he discovered the exact style of rope in the tack house that had been discovered at the scene of the crime. A forensic accounting was conducted on Dom's ranch records, and purchase orders for rope comparable to the one used to strangle the victim were noted on several occasions.

    And the last and most difficult detail to read was the report by the Travis County Crime Lab, indicating that, upon examination of Dom's Ford F-150 truck, several hairs matching Ms. Villarreal were discovered in the backseat and on the floorboard.

It was at this point that Callie began to cry uncontrollably. She had to log out of her computer and step away; these details were all too much to bear. As she stepped into her bedroom and fell onto the bed in tears, she remembered the intimate moments here, in this soft place, with Dom. This had to be a nightmare. It couldn't be real. There was no way she could fall so hard and so fast for someone who could do something so horrendous.

As the tears began to subside, she looked out the window, and glistening even brighter than usual were her two stars, Mike and Daddy. Calm immediately came over her, and a brief smile made its way to her face. Tears weren't going to help, and Callie's dad would have told her it was time to look at things with a fresh perspective. She had some contradictory evidence in her hand, and there must be something to that. It was time to decide what to do with it, which meant that it was time to bring Pam into the loop for some guidance.

"Hey, girlfriend! I was just thinking about checking on you. How are you holding up this week? I know trial is coming up soon, right?" Pam asked, in her usual cheerful voice.

"I'm hanging in there. Something else has happened, though, that I'm hoping you can give me some guidance on,"

Incredulity

Callie said, sighing slightly.

"Shoot! How can I help?"

Callie shared the information she'd gotten from the anonymous source, and Pam first responded by saying, "Wow, Callie! Do you have some sort of sign on your back that says, 'Follow me: I like trouble'?"

Callie laughed a second and said, "No, not a sign; just a magnet."

"Ha ha! Well, magnets are also great for attracting precious metals, right? But seriously, let's think this through. You have a few choices, in my mind. The first choice: You can throw it away, do nothing and pretend you didn't get it. Knowing you, that's probably already been something you thought of and dismissed. Choice number two: You could turn it over to -- well, never mind. We both know you can't do that. Choice number three: You can bring everything to me, and I can hang onto it. It can't be used as evidence, because we can't verify its authenticity, and we also don't know that it means anything at all. Brandon Brett is a decorated and well-respected officer, and this just isn't enough to go on a hunting expedition."

"Surely there's another option. I hate sitting on information that provides a glimmer of reasonable doubt about Dom's guilt. Couldn't we send the envelope to Dom's attorney?" Callie suggested.

"Well, you're putting the cart way before the horse, my friend. It could be that Dom's attorney already has this information. He's a stellar defense attorney, and I know for a fact he's got a private investigator who's very thorough. As your friend and your legal counsel, my best advice is to not touch the envelope and put it in a plastic baggie. We can meet next week for lunch at Chuy's, and I'll get it from you then."

"Okay," Callie agreed reluctantly. "I guess you're right. I really don't need more drama in my life at this point anyway."

"No, you don't, Sweetie. That's why I'm here. I'm the drama police," Pam replied with a giggle. "How's Wednesday of next week?"

"Perfect! Thanks, Pam. I'll see you on Wednesday around 12:15."

Almost as soon as Callie hung up the phone with Pam, she felt at ease. Pam was such a great friend, and she was level-headed. Of course, Callie normally was, but these circumstances were causing Callie's equilibrium to be completely off kilter. Vertigo didn't even come close to describing this feeling. Nonetheless, she had to let this new information sit and needed to regain her focus and composure for what was to come. "Hang on and hope for the best" was going to be the motto for the next few weeks.

It was definitely time for a relaxing bath, complete with

Incredulity

aromatherapy, soft music and lavender. Jerri, another friend of Callie's, had introduced her to the wonders of lavender. It was one of the few things that had been helpful when times were tough and the stress was at an all-time high. While the bath water was running, Callie filled the kettle with water for chamomile tea later and laid her favorite comfy pajamas on the bed.

Refreshed yet wonderfully relaxed, Callie fell into bed with her tea and a good book. Over the years of reading transcripts for proofing errors, it had become difficult for Callie to read for pleasure until she discovered audible books. Bedtime, hot tea and being read to by a deep male voice took her back to a time when she was a little girl, waiting for Daddy to come home from his law practice.

The sound of the words from the book drifted into the background as her thoughts brought forward a sweet memory of hearing her dad come in after she'd already gone to bed and was supposed to be sleeping. She got up and went into the kitchen, to his surprise. He'd said, "Baby Girl, what are you doing up?" She'd responded with, "I missed you, Daddy." He gave her a huge hug and said, "I missed you too. What if we have a date night, just the two of us? I'll put on some tea and warm some donuts in the oven, and we can catch up."

With three brothers who demanded his attention, it was hard for Callie to get much alone time with her dad. But there was nothing finer than warm donuts and hot tea with her dad, and the memory from that had been permanently impressed in her mind. He was gone now, and she still missed him terribly, but the memories of him and the love that they shared would always be there to bring a smile to Callie's face.

The sound of the words from the book came to the forefront again, but by that time, Callie had begun to feel as if she could finally put her brain to bed. Tomorrow would come early. She had about 400 pages left on one appeal transcript, with another 1,000-page appeal that had just been ordered. She'd need to be up by 4:00 a.m. if she was going to put a dent in those pages by the end of the day tomorrow. She pulled out her earbuds, pulled up the covers and fell soundly asleep.

The rest of the week was uneventful, thank goodness, and Callie was able to get the first appeal finished and make it through the testimony of the first few government witnesses of the next transcript. Finally, it was time for the weekend. Even though it would be a weekend of work, it was nice to be able to work from home. It would be a no-muss, no-fuss weekend. With Dom in lockup, Callie's life had gone back to what it was before. It had been so many weeks since she'd seen him, it felt like as if it never happened.

Obviously it did happen, but the reality was just too awful to dwell on at the moment. Shoving those thoughts out of her

Incredulity

mind and replacing them with a burger and something chocolate was happening, and then the computer would be her date for the rest of the weekend.

The weekend came and went quickly, which was normally the case when Callie was glued to her computer, but a little downtime on Sunday was a necessity. She hadn't talked to her children, Ali and Lauren, for several weeks because she was afraid her emotions would overtake her mouth and she'd blurt out everything to them. She wasn't willing to risk bringing them into this nightmare, and they didn't even know she was dating someone new. She'd bring them into the loop at some point after this was over, but for now, she just needed to hear their voices and check on the grandkids.

Whew! The phone call was a success, and neither Ali nor Lauren had suspected that anything was other than the norm in her life, but she'd kept the call short and focused on their lives and not hers. That was the easiest way to avoid any accidental slipup, and Callie could now get a few laps in and go out and grab a breakfast burrito from her favorite nearby taco stand.

There was a chill in the air this morning. It was a typical Austin fall day. The sun was glorious, and there wasn't a cloud in the sky, but it was a little too windy for the top to be down on the BMW. *What the heck,* Callie thought. She pulled her hair up and into a Longhorn ball cap she had and pushed the button to retract the top anyway. It was probably one of the last few times she'd get to enjoy the ride before the weather got too cold, and she needed to feel the wind in her face.

The taco stand was as busy as ever for a Sunday morning, but she'd stand in line for these burritos as long as it took to get one. They were mouthwatering and came with all of Callie's favorite ingredients: Eggs, fried potatoes and cheddar cheese, stuffed inside a made-from-scratch flour tortilla. Delish! She sat down at a picnic table with her burrito and coffee.

She could feel the warmth from the sun shining on the back of her neck, and that, combined with the first sip of fresh coffee and a bite of this amazing Tex-Mex delight was just the ticket to get the day going. Callie had made these on a regular basis for years for her family, but it was really a joy to have them prepared for her by someone else.

With breakfast finished, Callie decided to take the Beamer for a quick spin through the hills. It couldn't be a long drive, but she was feeling the need to take back a little power from the circumstances which were making her feel powerless. Rounding the curves at 65 miles an hour, hugging them with precision on every turn, hearing the whirring of the engine, and shifting gears was cathartic and exactly what she needed to get through the day's work and get ready for the upcoming week of a busy court docket. She'd be with Judge Goza this week, and he was a very

Incredulity

fast talker. She needed to get some machine practice time in before taking him on this week.

After a weekend of work, with 675 pages edited and sent off to the proofreader, Callie felt accomplished. She ate a quick sandwich for dinner and sat down at her steno machine for about an hour of practice, which went well. With that under her belt, she was finally free to relax with a movie and get ready for bed. It would be yet another early day in court. Judge Goza started court at 8:00. That was way too early for Callie and most of the lawyers, but he was the judge, so they showed up and pretended they liked it.

Callie got to the courthouse at 6:30 with an extra cup of coffee for herself. She wanted a tad more time to practice writing before getting into the courtroom, and she was also one of those people who thought that "on time" was really the definition of being late.

The day started out just as Callie had predicted... very fast! It was a great thing that she had enough experience in this business and with this judge to know that the practice really helped; otherwise, she would have been really struggling to keep up with him. The skilled stenographer was the equivalent of a professional athlete. In order to stay on top of the game, she had to practice on a regular basis, especially if she wasn't using her skill every day. Her mind and her muscles needed the exercise.

Kathy Zebert

It was a short docket today, which made for a great half day of editing. Callie was going to continue to stay focused and centered on her work this week. Her resolve was firm, and nothing was going to steer her off course. It was almost 5:30, and after one last trip to the rest room, it was time to hit the road for home.

Returning from the restroom, Callie grabbed her purse and computer and headed for the car, only to be waylaid by yet another envelope on her windshield. "Oh, my God! Stop it!" Callie exclaimed out loud. It was a good thing security had just walked to the other side of the parking lot, or he would have heard her and things could have gotten a lot more complicated. Callie simply pulled the envelope from underneath the wiper blade with a tissue and put it in a mailer she had in the backseat, deciding to ignore it. There was no way she was going to jump back on the rollercoaster from last week.

By the time she got about two miles down the road, though, Callie's curious nature won out. Rolling her eyes at having lost this battle, she turned into the nearest grocery store parking lot and pulled out another tissue to open the envelope. Oh, great! It was another key with a typed note: "Mailboxes, Etc., on Lamar, Box 205." This was getting to be ridiculous, and Callie was beginning to wonder if she was in some spy movie and someone forgot to pay her for her part.

Incredulity

Nonetheless, someone obviously wanted her to know more. But who? And why were they coming to her? Well, the answers may come later, but for now, she'd just run over to the Mailbox store and see what was next. It was in the opposite direction of home, but it would only take a few extra minutes.

Twenty minutes later, Callie arrived at the Mailboxes, Etc. store and went to the box. She retrieved the manila envelope inside with yet another tissue. She chuckled as she thought this might be a good time to take out stock in the tissue company. They were coming in handy for way more than sinus issues and wiping oil from her hands. She put the envelope in her purse and drove home, with a stop for an afternoon coffee.

Once inside the house, Callie sat down by the pool to enjoy her coffee and see what this new envelope contained. She opened it to reveal a thumb drive inside, with a short typed note on a piece of paper: "The pictures tell the story." Callie was grateful to be at home; she could get to the bottom of this in a few minutes. There was an old laptop in the closet that she never connected to the Internet, and she could easily wipe the hard drive on it, just cover her tracks, in case it was necessary.

Callie turned the closet light on and opened the door to retrieve the laptop from the top shelf. As she stepped forward to reach up, she kicked a box and looked down to see the boot box Dom had sent her in the first few weeks of their relationship. She stopped what she was doing, got down on her knees and opened the lid, revealing the boots. In an instant, the tears began to flow. She'd been trying to avoid thinking about her amazing cowboy and how much she loved him, and tears were counterproductive under the circumstances.

Up to this point, Callie had been doing a good job of numbing herself and robotically moving through the tasks of the day, but the emotional turmoil inside had been building for a while now, creating a weak spot in the dam Callie had built to contain her river of tears. The boots were the final breaking point, and the dam gave way as she began to sob.

It was at this moment that she realized that the tears she cried were not only okay, but they were necessary. The way her body expressed what her mind was feeling was through tears, and tears meant she had experienced great love and great loss. Callie was feeling both at that moment, plus the fear of the unknown. Her body ached to be held by Dom as she sat there in the floor of the closet, as she clutched the boots in her arms and remembered every wonderful moment of their time together.

The tears began to subside without Callie even realizing it, and surprisingly, she found she felt better. Remembering how much joy Dom had brought to her life had overcome the traumatizing events of the last few weeks. For the first time since Dom's arrest, Callie was 100 percent certain of his innocence, and

Incredulity

it only took allowing herself the gift of tears to get there. She was going to go get her cowboy back, and she was going to do it without losing everything else!

Completely resolved in mind and spirit, Callie got up from the floor, put on her beautiful boots, grabbed the laptop and fired it up. She left the dried tears on her face as a reminder of the love in her heart, and she went right back to her now-tepid coffee, poolside, and inserted the thumb drive. What came next was a confirmation of her renewed faith in Dom and her own keen sense of judgment.

The drive contained several dated folders. As she clicked to open each folder, there were a series of 8 x 10 photographs. They appeared to Callie to be professionally taken photographs. They weren't grainy like some cell phone photos could be; they were crystal clear, and they were each time and date stamped. She recognized Detective Brandon Brett in all of them, along with a woman. Each photograph was more and more provocative in nature, suggesting Brandon and this woman were more than friends.

Who was this woman? It wasn't Brandon's wife. Callie had met her several years ago, and she was a strikingly gorgeous redhead with flawless porcelain skin. This woman was just as beautiful, but looked to be younger, and either of Latino or Hispanic descent. The next obvious thought, since the last note seemed to imply that Brandon was somehow tied to the victim in Dom's case, was that this might be the victim.

Callie remembered her name was Angelina Villarreal, and a quick Google search with her cell phone confirmed Callie's suspicion about that. There was a write-up about the murder in the Statesman when it first happened, with a photo of Angelina. It was definitely her, and based on the photos on this thumb drive, Brandon seemed to be a little more involved than Callie had surmised earlier.

Reviewing the time and date stamps on the photos in comparison with the date of the young woman's murder, these were taken from about two months prior to the murder to just one day before the murder. And they were taken in locations all over Austin, showing Brandon and Angelina going in and out of seedy local motels and dive bars, including Boys Will Be Boys, where Angelina worked.

There was something to this, and Callie was so glad she was going to meet Pam for lunch tomorrow. This was worth looking into, especially coupled with the previous receipts. Everything seemed to point to Brandon Brett as a possible lead to something. Was it enough for someone to investigate further? Callie thought so, and apparently the anonymous sender thought so, but Pam would be a far better judge of that. For now, Callie was going to be patient and put this new information away for the

Incredulity

night. It was time for something chocolate. It had always been Callie's experience that patience was way more attainable when there was chocolate on the menu.

After a wonderful dose of patience, supplied by a warm mini chocolate lava cake and vanilla bean ice cream, Callie took a few extra laps in the pool, showered and got into bed; but not before reaching for a shirt Dom had left in her closet. As she put it on, she could smell the amazing scent of his aftershave and cologne as if he were right there with her, and comforted by that, she fell soundly asleep.

The next morning, Callie got out the door again by 6:00 a.m. Today was her last day with Judge Goza, and although he was not her favorite judge, she was looking forward to the day, merely because of her lunch with Pam. Lunch at Chuy's had become a regular treat for the two of them, and she couldn't wait to get a hug, get her Chuy's Elvis Chicken on, and share this new information with Pam.

The morning sentencing hearing flew by, and Callie raced out the door to her car. She was almost expecting another envelope, but there was nothing there. She wasn't sure whether to be grateful or disappointed, but regardless, she was anxious to get to lunch. When she walked in the door to Chuy's, she spotted Pam right away. She was waiting for her at a table in the back.

Pam was always easy to spot. She had the most amazing

smile of anyone Callie knew, and every time she saw her, Pam had that smile waiting. Pam was a totally put-together woman. She always wore stylish clothes, her nails were perfectly manicured, and her hair was the most beautiful shade of wheat-brown. She'd been married for 20 years to the same man, had two wonderful boys, and Callie had never, ever, seen nor heard her cry.

As she walked up to the table, Pam got up and hugged her so hard that Callie nearly lost her balance. They both laughed at the thought of Callie falling, and sat down to order. While they were waiting for their food, Callie handed over a spare satchel to Pam, telling her everything that she'd discovered the night before.

"Wow!" remarked Pam. "You're a popular girl, right?"

"I guess so," Callie said with a sigh. "Although this is one time I'd rather not be so popular. Part of me wishes whoever this is would leave me alone, but the other part of me sort of feels grateful for the information I'm getting. If I didn't have this information, my confidence in Dom would be really suffering right now, not to mention my self-confidence and my fear of all of this crashing down around me."

"Well, you're not to worry about that, my friend. I'm not going to let you lose everything. It's not going to happen. Trust me?"

"Implicitly," Callie replied, nodding.

Right on cue, the server put the hot plate of queso-

Incredulity

smothered Elvis Chicken, refried beans and Mexican rice in front of Callie, and the endorphins kicked in with the first bite. Pam had her favorite, the Mexi-Cobb salad, which was obviously the healthier option, but Callie needed the endorphins more than Pam did at this point.

The topic of conversation switched to Pam and her life, because Callie really needed to talk about something other than this drama that was consuming every brain cell of hers. Pam talked about her boys and the new school year activities, and her second honeymoon to Brazil over the summer. It was nice just to talk about something normal for a few minutes, and Callie was grateful to Pam for the temporary distraction.

After the plates were cleared from the table, however, Pam brought the conversation back to Callie's conundrum. Pam's plan was really no different than she had with the first envelope Callie had given her. She was going to take it back to her office and keep it with the rest of the documents. There still wasn't really enough to open an investigation of Brandon, because they didn't know if this was from a reliable source.

"Callie, these photos could have come from anywhere. And without knowing more, we just can't risk turning it over and possibly exposing your part in all of this. I do think it's enough, though, to let my investigator take a look without raising any red flags."

Kathy Zebert

"Well, that's one step closer to doing something than before. It's killing me that I can't for the life of me figure out who's behind these notes and why they sought me out as the person to give them to."

"You've got to be patient and let all of this unfold. Whatever happens, you need to protect yourself. Things typically work out the way they're supposed to, Callie. I don't have to tell you that. You've lived longer than I have."

"Yes," Callie said with a laugh, "long enough to know all the answers but forget all the questions."

The two laughed out loud as Callie paid the check, and after that point, they both left for the parking lot and said their good-byes. It was time to get back to the afternoon court session, with two final plea hearings. Pam had reassured Callie that she'd keep her posted on anything that the investigator uncovered, and that was all it took to get her through another day.

After two 20-minute plea hearings, it was time for a coffee break, a quick trip to the bathroom, and the rest of the afternoon to, yet again, edit transcripts. Editing was such a time-consuming task, especially on large appeals, and the best way to stay motivated to finish several hundred pages came from as a suggestion from Callie's dad. One day during a conversation with him about how exhausted she was from editing, he'd said to her, "Count dollars, Baby Girl, not pages." The visual from this was

Incredulity

an easy motivational trick. At the end of the hour, she could quickly do the math in her head and challenge herself to get a higher dollar count in the next hour. *Thanks, Daddy, for yet another one of life's gems,* Callie thought to herself, as she dove right in to editing.

Finally, at 5:30, with lots of dollars counted, Callie shut her laptop down and headed for home. She was looking forward to a little R&R and a massage she'd booked over the weekend. The entire weekend was going to be Callie. She knew she needed every ounce of rejuvenation of mind and body in order to get through the next week, and a spa day was just the right way to start.

On the drive home, her thoughts drifted back to Dom. She wondered what he was thinking and how he was feeling. She hadn't been able to talk to him, to hold him, to reassure him, nothing. Her pain was immeasurable, but for the first time, she began to think about his pain. Although she felt confined by the circumstances, she was at least free to enjoy a cup of coffee, a comfortable bed, and her freedom. He didn't have any of those things.

Two things were for sure, though. He still had her heart and she was doing everything in her power to help him. When she sat down by the pool and put her toes in the water, the sun had begun to set. In the quiet beauty of the next few moments, she could nearly hear the sound of his voice as he sang the song he'd written for her. No other man had ever touched her soul in the way he had. The love that they felt couldn't be put into words. And remembering the words to that song, she imagined him seeing the same sunset and gently whispered, "The sunset will bring you back to me, Dom. I love you."

The evening turned into morning, and the morning turned into two days later. Keeping busy was so crucial for Callie, with the trial set to begin on Monday. The plans were already in place to treat herself to an entire day at the spa on Saturday, with a trip to San Marcos on Sunday for some shoe shopping, completed by dinner on the grill at home and peach cobbler for dessert. This was a stress-free zone now, and Callie was ready for the battle of her life.

Chapter 7: The Silent Heroine

The first day of Dom's trial finally came, and the jury pool was going to be in around 8:30 a.m. Callie set out for the courthouse a little earlier than usual, with a stop for Judge Hamilton's special coffee. The one shining star this week was going to be having him sit on the bench for this case. Even though she couldn't share the details of her very difficult circumstances, having someone kind and easy to work with gave her some solace. He was also the most respectful and knowledgeable member of the judiciary in the district, which would ensure Dom got a fair trial.

Judge Hamilton smiled as he reached for his coffee and looked down at Callie. "How's my favorite court reporter this morning? Thank you, as always, for the wonderful coffee. It looks like it's going to be a hard week for us." He clearly had no idea what an understatement that was, Callie thought, and she simply replied, "Looks like it. So glad the coffee made you smile."

Callie was set up and ready to go by 8:00 a.m., the prosecutor and defense attorney arrived a few minutes later, and the deputies brought Dom in and removed his cuffs. As he made his way across the courtroom to the defense table, Callie's pulse began to race. He was in his gray pinstripe suit with a cornflower button-down shirt and the tie she'd bought for him in Ruidoso.

Kathy Zebert

Callie began to feel breathless, so she took a deep breath and looked up at the ceiling. She'd heard a tip many years ago that if you looked at the ceiling, it was nearly impossible for tears to show in your eyes. It definitely did the trick. She'd decided at this point that it would be important to remain focused on the large portrait in the back of the courtroom for the entirety of the trial. She couldn't bear to look in Dom's eyes.

Judge Hamilton asked for the jury panel to be escorted to the courtroom from the jury assembly room, and 50 were brought in and seated in the gallery. Voir dire went very quickly, surprisingly, and a jury of 12 plus two alternates were sworn and seated in the box by 10:30. After a 10-minute break, opening statements began. Callie made it through the voir dire, but opening statements were going to be difficult.

Stepping out the back door of the courthouse for a few minutes, Callie looked up to the heavens and began to say a prayer out loud. She needed every ounce of her faith to get through this. If she could make it through the first day, the dust would settle and she could maintain her composure for the rest of the week. Feeling slightly calmer, she waited in the hallway until she saw Judge Hamilton walking towards the courtroom. She took her seat and pulled up her machine just before he took the bench.

"Mr. Farber, ready for your opening statement?"

Incredulity

"Yes, Your Honor."

"All right, sir. You may proceed."

As Mr. Farber began his opening statement, Callie listened very carefully to the facts the State intended to prove in its case in chief. Normally, these facts had no impact on her and were merely words upon words that she'd heard too many times to count. Today was different. The words she heard today affected her life and the life of the man she'd fallen in love with.

Mr. Farber gave his usual eloquent, matter-of-fact opening statement, with the final statement, "We believe that in light of all of the evidence we will put before you, we'll be able to prove to you, beyond a reasonable doubt, that the defendant, Dominic Jaxson, is guilty of the charge of murder in the first degree, as charged in the indictment." He then thanked the jury for their service and sat down.

"Mr. Spence, opening statements?"

"Yes, Your Honor. Thank you," Mr. Spence began.

"Ladies and gentlemen of the jury, the case being brought against my client, Dominic Jaxson, is one of strictly circumstantial evidence. The judge will explain that term to you later on in the trial, but for now, it's basically a series of circumstances leading a reasonable person to believe a crime has been committed by a specific person, but it's not a concrete proof, such as perhaps an eyewitness who personally watched a crime happen right in front of them."

As Callie listened, she was hoping to hear something about the information she'd received, but to her disappointment, there was nothing. Not a single word about the possibility that Brandon Brett could have been involved somehow. But then the thought occurred to her that he could use it later, for impeachment, because she knew Brandon would be on the stand as the first witness.

Mr. Spence continued, "We believe the proof will show that Mr. Jaxson is a well-respected member of the Metro Austin community, a graduate of the University of Texas, and has never been in any sort of trouble whatsoever, and couldn't possibly have committed this heinous crime against this young woman. My client had no reason to commit the crime charged. He didn't even know this poor young woman. They were simply acquaintances and had only seen each other a few times. We believe after hearing all of the evidence, you will find my client not guilty of this crime."

As he sat down, Callie felt the urge to stand up and shout, "Is that it? That's your defense? He's a Longhorn alumnus? Sure, because no graduate from Texas ever committed murder. Pam had said this guy was an outstanding lawyer, but Callie hadn't seen him before and wondered if they were talking about the same person.

Incredulity

Things weren't looking good so far, but as with every criminal trial Callie had ever been involved in, there was sure to be a surprises here and there. She had often been 100 percent convinced that the defendant committed a crime, right up until the defense put on its side of the case. Perhaps this lawyer was pretending to have no evidence and would use it in another way. Callie was in a perfect position to watch, like it or not. So she decided to give him the benefit of the doubt, because, well, she had no choice.

"Thank you, Mr. Spence."

"Ladies and gentlemen, it's now maybe a little earlier than I normally take lunch, but this is a good time for us to break. Please be back in the jury assembly room no later than 1:00 so that we can begin with the testimony of the first State witness. Please do not discuss the case with each other or allow anyone to discuss the case with you."

The jury left the courtroom and court was adjourned until 1:00. Callie stepped out of the courtroom quickly, because she was just shy of screaming and needed to calm herself. As she rounded the corner hurriedly, she nearly ran into Dominic. She stepped to the side to avoid a full-on collision, but not before their arms touched, causing their eyes to meet. For a full five seconds, they stared longingly at each other without saying a word, which the deputy didn't notice because he was staring at one of the young female clerks nearby.

"Excuse us, Callie," said the deputy.

"Totally my fault," Callie replied. "I'm in a hurry to run a few errands on the lunch break."

Callie immediately turned her eyes to the floor and all but sprinted to the parking lot. If she could just make it to her car, she could let out a scream. And she did: a blood-curdling one. After that, she felt better. The trial was only going to be one week, after all, and half of a day was nearly over. She could do it, and she could do it with grace.

Lunch away was a great idea, and she made it back to court by 12:45. That was just enough time to freshen up in the bathroom and get a bottled water for the afternoon, and not enough time to think about anything other than that. After a deep breath, Callie opened the courtroom door and went straight for her spot in the room, eyes locked on the portrait of some white-haired judge on the back wall.

Judge Hamilton asked the bailiff to bring in the jury. Once they were seated, he asked, "Is the State ready to call its first witness?"

"Yes, Your Honor. We call Detective Brandon Brett."

Brandon was called from the lobby of the courthouse, and he came in, was sworn and took the stand. Callie internally rolled her eyes as she always did when he took the stand, but this time

Incredulity

she really felt it. Her impressions of him had been confirmed over the last couple of weeks, and she was hoping the jury would either hear something about that now.

It was about that time that Callie noticed that the courtroom door opened and someone came in. The woman looked familiar. Callie had seen her somewhere and was trying to place her. After a few minutes of blah, blah, blah about Brandon's background as a stellar police officer, it dawned on Callie where she knew this woman from. It was Brandon's wife, June.

They'd met at a staff Christmas party several years ago. June was a tall, beautiful, refined young woman. They'd had lunch a time or two before Mike died, but she hadn't seen her since his passing. June had a very sweet spirit about her, but there was always a certain sadness in her eyes. As June caught Callie's glance, she smiled, but the sadness was still there. She'd not noticed her in court before, but then again, her eyes were almost never towards the back of the courtroom.

Brandon's testimony was just as she expected it to be, because it was basically recalling from his report. She was sure he studied it just before coming to court. And he was as arrogant as usual. He'd shaved his head since the last time Callie saw him. She was sure that was because he had a huge bald spot in the crown. Hopefully, the jury would ignore everything he said on direct and see only his cocky attitude.

Kathy Zebert

When the direct examination of Brandon was finished, it was time for Mr. Spence to cross-examine. Here we go! If there was ever a time to hit him with everything, it was now. Callie anxiously waited for Mr. Spence to bring up the photos, the receipts, the rope, but again, nothing. The cross-examination consisted of, "Is it possible that the hair could have been there at a time before this murder?" and "How many other people could have bought this rope?"

There were a few things that put a tiny shred of reasonable doubt in there, but nothing compelling, and the evidence against Dominic was pretty solid. The one constant thing Callie had noticed about juries sitting on cases that involved a heinous crime was this: The jury wanted someone to be punished, and that was usually going to be the person sitting in that defendant's chair, unless the State had little to no evidence to convict them. And the State wasn't going to spend the money to bring someone to trial if they didn't have a really great case.

There was no redirect, as Mr. Spence really didn't have a strong cross-examination. Callie was completely devastated at this point. It didn't look good for Dom. As Brandon stepped down from the stand and the medical examiner was called, Callie couldn't help but feel defeated. She reminded herself, though, that the case wasn't over until there was a verdict, and justice nearly always prevailed. More patience, aka chocolate, was on the

Incredulity

menu for tonight... and lots and lots of prayers.

The medical examiner really was there to confirm the cause and time of death. Dr. Tanner was the medical examiner, and he was rarely, if ever, wrong on either of those. He was a Harvard graduate with 25 years of experience, and state-of-the-art equipment at his fingertips. Nothing clearing Dom was going to come from his testimony.

"Counsel, is this a good time for our afternoon break?" interjected Judge Hamilton.

"It's perfect timing, Your Honor," responded Mr. Farber.

"All right, Ladies and Gentlemen of the Jury. Let's take our afternoon break. There are refreshments in the jury assembly room for you. Please don't go too far, as I'd like to stay on track for today. We'll be adjourning this afternoon at about 4:00, because I've got a meeting to attend outside of the courthouse."

As the jury was excused, Callie went to grab a quick cup of coffee and a protein bar from her office. She was getting that afternoon fog in her brain, and she wanted to stay as alert as possible for the rest of the day. It was all that she could do to manage a fake smile throughout the rest of the day, but it was almost over. One day down, even though it had been a long and disappointing one.

After the jury returned, the next State's witness was called. It was a witness who had seen Dom and Ms. Villarreal arguing on the night before her body was found. Mr. Spence made quick work of casting doubt on his testimony, because the witness didn't have any idea what the argument was about, only that it appeared to be heated. And it was in a dark and smoky bar setting, with tons of people between them. Score at least one for Dom's defense. But was it enough? Maybe not, especially when considered with all of the other evidence from the Dom's truck, the ranch, and his business computer.

The State's witnesses were finished for the day, but the forensic accountant and crime lab analyst would be the final nails in Dom's coffin if there wasn't some rabbit Mr. Spence could pull out of his trusty cowboy hat. Yes, he wore one too. Callie had noticed it sitting on top of the briefcase that was lying on the floor beside him.

At about 4:40, the jury was excused, with the judge's admonitions not to talk about the case or read about it or do any research on their own. There were no motions or discussions to be had by the attorneys, and Judge Hamilton left the bench.

Callie couldn't get out of the building fast enough. There was a glass of wine with her name on it at home. She packed up her laptop and left the courtroom for the parking lot. There were people walking through the parking lot, and as she exchanged pleasantries with them and went to open her door, it was then that she noticed that all-too-familiar white envelope on her

Incredulity

windshield.

    She sighed deeply and closed her eyes, thinking to herself that whatever this was didn't really even matter. Neither of the other envelopes amounted to anything that would help. What was the point of any of this? Using yet another tissue, she removed the envelope, got in the car and thought, *what the heck?* She might as well take a look. Even if it hadn't helped so far, it couldn't hurt either.

    Inside the envelope was a key to a new mailbox place, this time to a place she was unfamiliar with on Bee Cave Road. There was no note this time, but the key had a tag indicating that the box number was 426. Callie knew the general area of the store, and it was on her way home, so off she went, hoping for some miracle.

    She pulled up to the store just as it was about to close and quickly retrieved the envelope inside. There was no cryptic phrase on the note this time; it was only a link to some random Web address. Callie was too exhausted to think about what any of this meant for now, so she put the car in drive and continued home to greet that glass -- and maybe after that, two glasses -- of wine.

    The work clothes and heels were definitely being substituted for jeans, a T-shirt and Callie's favorite pair of running shoes. The envelope was lying on the coffee table, but

Kathy Zebert

Callie ignored it, going for the wine closet. She perused the selection, but nothing sounded good. She opened the patio door and felt the chill in the air that she hadn't noticed on her way in. This was the perfect time for a cup of cocoa instead, and it fit the bill for both the chocolate and the drink.

The pool had been covered today by the pool service, but there was wood in the outdoor fireplace, which made the perfect setting for her cocoa. There was something so relaxing about cocoa, crackling oak and the warmth of the flames. Staring into the red-orange of the fire was mesmerizing for a moment, and the disappointment of the day was nearly forgotten. But then, just as quickly as she'd forgotten, she remembered again.

She sat there, still, for the next two hours, refusing to get up and get that envelope. No matter how hard she tried, though, the pull to find out the significance of that Web site drew her to the envelope like a magnet. She picked up her purse, carefully placed the envelope into it and drove over to the local Internet café, which was open late.

When Callie drove up, the place was empty except for a couple of guys behind the counter. She went to the back to one of the computers, signed on as a guest and paid with a gift card she'd been saving for something special. This certainly qualified as special, she thought to herself.

She typed in the Web address and put her earbuds in, and

Incredulity

a screen popped up asking for a password, which she found on the note. It took her to a series of MPEG videos, the dates of which spanned from May up to the current day. She clicked on the most recent one, and it looked similar to the surveillance videos she'd seen in trials before, but based on the time/date stamp, it was a live feed from inside a car.

She said quietly to herself, but out loud, "What is this? Where is this? Whose car is" – hold the phone, Callie! This was Dom's truck. But it couldn't be; his truck was in the impound lot, and it had been there since Dom was arrested. Even so, it was definitely his truck. She recognized the ranch logo Dom had imprinted on the dashboard.

The next obvious step was to begin with the first video from back in May. The video must have been voice and/or motion sensitive, because Callie could hear Dom's voice and see the back of his head. "This is DEA Operative 31420, Field notes follow. Undercover investigation into Operation Cobra out of Austin PD. Assignment, Day 1, on target for trip to Mexico for a load to be delivered to a private farm owned by Detective Brandon Brett."

Whoa! This was real. Callie's cowboy was a DEA agent, and she had no idea. How did she not pick up on this? She could usually spot these guys in the hallway of the courthouse. He was really great at his job. For Callie, this was both a relief and a disappointment. A relief, because it meant he wasn't about to commit a crime, unless it was an accident. A disappointment, because he had deceived her, leaving her to doubt the authenticity of their relationship.

Nonetheless, the more important date would be the date and time of the murder, since there wasn't time to look at all of these. She clicked out of that video and on to the video time stamped at around 2:00 a.m., about 45 minutes before the medical examiner's estimated time of death. Opening that video led her to the most gruesome thing she'd ever seen. Dom wasn't on this video; it was Brandon and Ms. Villarreal. Callie cranked up the volume so that she didn't miss a word.

"So why are you in your boy's truck?" asked Angelina.

"His truck was blocking mine, and he was passed out on the couch, so I borrowed it," said Brandon, a smirk on his face.

"Nice ride. So are we agreed, then, Baby? You're going to leave your wife so we can get married?"

"I thought about it, but we're going to have to wait. She'll take everything if I leave now. You just have to be patient."

"Patience is for losers, Baby. I hold all the cards. I told you that your boy is a fed and wants me to roll over on you. I also told you that the only way I don't do that is if you leave your wife. I ain't playing."

"You know I love you, Angel," pleaded Brandon. "If you love me, you'll wait and let me figure this out."

Incredulity

"I love you, but I'm done playing your little game. I deserve to be in that big white house, not her. I'm not staying in the motel anymore. Either you're with me or you're in jail. Either way, you're not with her."

At that point, Brandon pulled the truck into an alleyway, put it in park and slid over in the seat next to Angelina and began to kiss her, reaching over into the backseat of the crew cab and grabbing the lasso. With a quick flick of his wrist, the rope was around Angelina's neck. Callie heard a snap and saw Angelina's body go limp in the seat.

Brandon got out, opened the passenger door, removed the rope from Angelina's neck, picked her up and dropped her into the Dumpster a few feet away. He then threw the rope into the nearby drain and got back into the truck, parking it in the same position Dom had left it in earlier. He got into his car and took off.

After seeing all of this, Callie couldn't move. The details of this horrible crime against this young woman would stay with her for the rest of her life. She felt sick, but she knew this was the evidence that would clear Dom. She had to get it to the right people. She cleared the history and the cache on the computer, walked out the door and immediately got the burner phone out of the glove box where she'd last left it.

"Pam, I know it's late, but I need you and your investigator to meet me right now."

"I'm on my way. Are you okay, Callie? What's going on?"

"I've found a miracle," Callie said, almost breathless. "Can you meet me in the parking lot of the truck stop off the interstate in Selma?"

"I'll be there in 45 minutes," said Pam.

"Okay. Bring your investigator and a laptop."

Callie made it to the truck stop first, which gave her an opportunity for all of this to sink in. Dom could be free by tomorrow, if all of this worked the way she wanted it to. But what if they wouldn't let this evidence in? She couldn't think about that. They just had to. He didn't do it, and this was clear evidence. Plus, she knew the chain of custody hadn't been broken, because Dom's truck had never left the impound lot.

After a few minutes, Pam drove up, followed by her investigator, Paul, and they got into Callie's car. Paul opened up his laptop and navigated to the pertinent video, and both Paul and Pam had the same reaction Callie did. Pam had to get out of the car and walk it off, because she was visibly shaken. Although Paul was used to seeing the darker side of life on a regular basis, he'd never actually seen a murder take place on camera and just sat there with a stunned look on his face. But time was of the essence, and he assured Callie that he would get this to the investigator in Dom's case within the hour. It just so happened that they'd been

Incredulity

buddies for years.

Paul left with the envelope a few minutes later, and Pam got back into the car with Callie. The two sat there, holding hands, with their eyes closed. Seeing something so brutal happen, not knowing it was coming and not being able to stop it, was just about the worst thing either of them had ever experienced. Hearing about the horrible things people do to each other was bad enough after the fact, but both Callie and Pam had become somewhat desensitized to it in order to function in their professional roles. Watching it happen and being so personally invested in the situation was completely different, and it was something no one could have prepared them for, but sharing the experience made it easier for both of them to deal with.

An hour later, Callie and Pam got out of the car and hugged each other tight, sharing tears wrapped up in so many different emotions. The circumstances of the last six weeks had taken a toll on Callie's positive spirit. She'd maintained her grace throughout, for the most part, but she felt as if she'd been through a natural disaster.

No property was destroyed, and the physical things around her were still intact, but her peace of mind had been shattered into a million tiny pieces. It would take some time to gather those pieces up and carefully place them back together. Still, Callie knew that this traumatic experience, just as every other in her life, would change how she viewed the world. For now, the only thing on her mind was getting her life back: her cowboy, the freedom to walk around without being under the microscope, and the ability to put on a smile that was authentic.

Back at home around midnight, Callie got out the lavender salts and poured them into a hot bath. It was going to be difficult to sleep, but she really needed to be rested for tomorrow. She hadn't been this anxious since she gave birth to Lauren. These feelings were not foreign to her, but Callie had never done well when she couldn't control an outcome. It was extremely difficult to just be still and watch as events unfolded, even with a strong and steadfast faith in God's plan. Her grandma used to say, "We give all of our problems to God in prayer, but then we want to take them back." Truer words were never spoken.

The lavender really did the trick, and Callie's body was completely relaxed. Her brain, however, wouldn't be tamed. Every time she closed her eyes, the vision of Brandon strangling Angelina appeared behind her eyelids. Frustrated and knowing she had to get some sleep, she finally decided to get up and take some melatonin. It had helped with the insomnia after her dad died, and she knew how it affected her body. She took one with a bottled water, and 15 minutes later, she was out cold.

Morning finally came, and Callie was anxious to get the day started. She made her regular coffee stop and got into the

Incredulity

courtroom earlier than usual, expecting to see some crazier-than-usual activity. At about 8:15, Mr. Farber and Mr. Spence, along with their investigators, came walking in almost simultaneously, and a minute later, Judge Hamilton walked in the back door and stepped onto the bench.

"I understand we have something to discuss before we bring in the jury?"

In an excited voice, Mr. Spence jumped up and said, "Yes, Your Honor."

"I'll hear you, Mr. Spence."

"May it please the Court, at around 1:30 this morning, I got a call from my investigator about new exculpatory evidence which completely exonerates my client, Mr. Jaxson. I called my learned colleague, Mr. Farber, and he and I met my investigator, Simon Harper, at his office to review the evidence."

Judge Hamilton interrupted and asked, "Wait a minute. What's this evidence?"

Mr. Spence replied, "It's a surveillance video of the murder, Your Honor."

Where did this video come from, and why are we just now hearing about it?" asked Judge Hamilton, an irritated tone in his voice.

"I was just getting to that, Judge. This video was discovered by another investigator, Paul Schuster, in an unrelated case and then handed off to my investigator, Mr. Harper, once it was determined what it was. I believe Your Honor is familiar with both of these investigators and their reputations as professionals."

Judge Hamilton responded, "I am. What does the State say, Mr. Farber?"

"Your Honor, we object to this coming in at this late hour of the trial. We don't know the original source behind this so-called lead."

"Mr. Spence, do you know the source?"

"No, Your Honor. But in my estimation, the source doesn't matter, because the video was recorded by a surveillance video camera inside Mr. Jaxson's car, which has been in the Austin Police Department impound lot since the day of his arrest. They supposedly did a thorough search of the vehicle, and while they didn't uncover the video camera, they certainly had every opportunity to. The chain of custody hasn't been broken, and we believe this evidence is admissible as exculpatory evidence, and should be considered in the light most favorable to Mr. Jaxson."

Mr. Farber began to respond with, "Well, if Your Honor please –" but Judge Hamilton cut him off.

"Just a minute, Mr. Farber. Has anybody been to the impound lot to take another look at this vehicle?"

"No, Your Honor. We got this so late, we haven't had an

Incredulity

opportunity to get over there," Mr. Farber replied.

"Well, I'm not making a ruling on this until we find that camera and I've seen the video. I don't like to waste jury time, but I'll let them know there will be a delay in court this morning. I expect you to be quick about it, though," Judge Hamilton said sternly before he abruptly stepped down from the bench and out of the courtroom.

Dom hadn't been brought to the courtroom, so Callie was wondering if he even knew about the turn of events in his favor. She was hoping there wasn't going to be some legal finagling, causing a snag in the process. She'd worked so hard and waited for so long for this nightmare to end, and she wasn't sure she could take another negative surprise.

An hour later, court was back in session, and the camera had been found. It had been hidden in the dome light of Dom's truck. When they'd found the other evidence in the truck, they apparently thought they had enough to convict Dom and ended the vehicle search. That turned out to be a huge mistake on the State's part. If they'd found that, none of this ever would have happened. But given the fact that the lead investigator on the case was the actual perpetrator of the crime, it probably would have ended up being destroyed.

Judge Hamilton returned to the bench and said, "Counsel, while you've been conducting your search of the defendant's vehicle, I've been busy myself. I got a call from the DEA, with a request to review the videos with us. Over to my right is Special Agent Frank Kendrick with the DEA."

Callie was taken aback, and Mr. Farber looked confused. Dom's attorney must have known everything about Dom's undercover assignment because he didn't even flinch. Dom was entering the courtroom, and Callie finally felt comfortable enough to make eye contact with him in the courtroom. His eyes widened and he smiled a little as he was led to his chair next to Mr. Spence.

"All right. Let's see what's on these videos, shall we?" began Judge Hamilton."

The videos were played, one by one, until the murder. Callie turned her eyes away from that one. She didn't need to see that one again, as it was permanently branded into her mind at this point. All of the videos leading up to the point of the murder consecutively and succinctly outlined Dom's investigation into Brandon Brett's illegal drug smuggling activities, and all the parties were in agreement that Dominic should be released.

"Mr. Jaxson, you are free to go about your day, with the apologies of this Court and an expectation that the State will remove any and all records associated with your arrest, to be outlined in the form of an order which will be on my desk and signed by me at the end of the day. We owe you a debt of gratitude

Incredulity

for your service to this country, this state and to us personally. You, and others like you, help to keep our system free from corruption, which is the only way we can maintain the public trust."

The CSO was instructed by Judge Hamilton to leave Dominic in the courtroom, process him out immediately and bring his personal effects to him. A bench warrant was issued for Brandon Brett. Callie surmised that the rest of his life would be spent in both state and federal custody, which he totally deserved.

With everyone still in place and Dom waiting to be released, the jury was brought back. Judge Hamilton simply told them that certain facts had come to light which exonerated the defendant. He excused them and thanked them for their valuable service as jurors and announced court in recess, stepping off the bench.

Callie wasn't quite sure where to go at this point. She sat there for a few minutes and watched as Dom was handed his personal effects. As he got up to leave the courtroom, he gave Callie a huge smile and nod while no one was looking. Even though the case was over, it was too soon to reveal anything about their relationship. She did, however, manage a smile, and he turned to walk out the back door of the courtroom. Finally, it was over, and life could begin again.

The courtroom was quiet, and Callie finally felt free to

move... somewhere, but where? The case was over, and she really wanted to fall into Dom's arms, but she still had work to do. She wasn't sure she was going to be able to pull that off, but she would give it her best shot. There would be time for a reunion with Dom later, and she was sure he needed some time alone.

Finally to her feet, Callie walked out of the courtroom, turning to smile at this room where lives were judged and fates were decided every day. Over the course of 15 years, Callie had been impacted by so many of the cases, but as an impartial guardian of the record. Today, she could truly empathize. She felt the turmoil of the families behind the defendants. She felt the pain of the victims of circumstances beyond their control. And fortunately, she felt the joy of triumph, vindication and true justice.

As she moved out the door and down the hall past Judge Hamilton's office, Callie saw him sitting at his desk. He looked up as she was passing and said, "Callie, can I see you for a second." Callie paused, thinking to herself that she must be in trouble because he never asked to "see her" in that way.

Of course, she said, "Sure, Judge," and stepped into his office, at which point he asked her to close the door and sit down. Then she really knew something was up, and that impulse to run snuck up on her like a thief in the night. She slowly closed the door and sat down, afraid of what was coming next.

Incredulity

Judge Hamilton simply said, "I know, Callie."

Callie then asked, "Know what, Judge?"

"Everything," he replied.

That one word was really all it took to let her know that her secret was no longer a secret. She was overwhelmed by guilt and fear, and just knew she was going to be fired. She'd done everything in her power to keep this from happening. Her hands had been tied, and this juggling act she'd performed very well so far was about to end with all of the balls on his office floor.

Just when Callie's anxiety was about to get the best of her, Judge Hamilton said, "I called you in here to tell you how proud I am of you." What did he just say? Did she hear correctly? He was proud? Then she thought the next word out of his mouth was going to be "but." To her surprise, that word never came. In fact, it was quite the opposite.

"You are my favorite court reporter. You know that, right? And even though you may believe it's because you bring me coffee, that's not it. You are such a sweet spirit, and you care so much about the system, the record, and the people who walk into that courtroom. I've watched as you dealt with two major losses in your life, and even at your darkest, you never stopped smiling or caring. Your moral and ethical compasses are above reproach, and I'm so proud that I get to have you by my side in that courtroom."

Kathy Zebert

The unexpected reaction by this man that she respected immensely brought tears to the corners of Callie's eyes and they began streaming uncontrollably down her cheeks. She was embarrassed because she'd never cried in front of him before, but what happened next turned that embarrassment into comfort. Judge Hamilton got up from his desk, sat down next to Callie on the sofa and hugged her tightly, saying, "All is well, Callie."

If anyone had ever told her that her boss would be hugging her, she would have laughed and told them they were nuts. *He's not the hugging type,* she'd always thought. And these days, everyone was worried about sexual harassment lawsuits, so hugging wasn't something that was deemed appropriate professional behavior, especially not in the courthouse setting.

Callie wasn't one to beg off a hug when she needed one, though, and this one was special. This felt like a hug from Daddy, and she really needed one right now. The longer he hugged, the more Callie cried, until she was finished, at which point he let go and smiled the biggest smile she'd ever seen on his face.

As Judge Hamilton stood up, he said, "Go home, Callie, and don't come back until after Thanksgiving. The docket is light, and I believe you have some thanks to be giving, and some laughter and love to share." Callie knew better than to argue with a judge, and he was right. She needed to love, to heal, give thanks, and she desperately needed to see her cowboy.

Incredulity

As she walked out of the judge's office, she turned to say, "Judge, can you keep a secret?"

He looked up and said with a wink, "Not as well as you."

"Ha ha! Probably not. But I just wanted to tell you that you're my favorite judge. Don't tell Judge Goza, though. He may decide to take it out on me and talk faster."

"Your secret is safe with me, Callie."

Stepping out of that office was completely different than stepping in, and Callie could feel a little spring in her step. She picked up her things from her office and ran down the hallway to the car. Life and Dom were waiting.

Chapter 8: Trailblazing

Pam was on Callie's speed dial, and she couldn't call her fast enough. She thought maybe someone would have stolen her thunder by calling Pam, but to her delight, she hadn't been told anything about the outcome of Dom's trial. Even if she had, Callie wanted to give a verbal thanks, though there was no way she'd ever be able to thank her enough for all that she'd done.

Pam picked up the phone and anxiously asked, "Well?"

Callie replied, "Everything worked out perfectly, Pam, thanks to you," filling in the details of the morning.

"I can't tell you how thrilled I am for you, Callie. It was a long road to get here, but you made it."

Callie added, "No. We made it. I could never have done this without you. In a few days, I want to plan a girl's trip for just the two of us. My treat."

Pam said, "Of course, you know I'm always up for a party. Call me in a few days. Go get your guy back. Love you!"

"Love you too, Pam!" Callie said, as she hung up.

The next call would be to Dom, and although she wanted to hear his voice, she decided to text him to meet her instead. That way, she could get home, change clothes, wash the black lines of mascara off her cheeks and look her best for her guy.

She pulled off the road to send a quick text to Dom and

Incredulity

waited for a reply. It was going to be as quick as she could manage, so it would need to be loving, but to the point.

"Sunset's calling, me and you. Shenanigans, 4:30 p.m.?"

And the response came through about four seconds later.

"Already there, impatiently waiting."

Callie hadn't felt her heart race this way since she and Dom had been together at the cabin in Ruidoso. That seemed like a lifetime ago, and she knew that there would be hurdles to get over to get their relationship back on track. It could never go back to the way it was before, but that was a good thing. Love is supposed to get better with time and experience in a relationship, and when she thought about how much they'd come through so far, the future seemed to be an easy downhill coast.

But in order for the relationship to rekindle, she'd actually have to see him first. So off she sped, just daring a police officer to pull her over. She made it home in record time, showered, changed into black jeans, a sexy, off-the-shoulder red sweater and her custom red boots, put her hair up and spritzed on Dom's favorite perfume.

On her way out the door, grabbed her overnight bag with all of her essentials in it, because she had a feeling she might need it. Twenty minutes later, she pulled into the empty parking lot of Shenanigans. All she saw was Dom's BMW and two other cars. It was odd that no one was there, because the place was famous for their views of the sunset. Despite that, she shrugged the thought off and went inside. She opened the door to find the lights turned down, as if the place was closed. What was going on?

About the time that popped into her head, the song Dom had written for her began to play over the sound system, and he came walking down the stairs from the upper deck to greet her. He never looked as good as he did in this moment. It was as if she was seeing him for the first time, but with a new set of eyes; the eyes of love.

He took her into his arms and kissed her tenderly on the lips, and every ounce of anxiety, doubt and sadness was replaced by sheer breathless joy. Dom said, "Callie, I'm so sorry I –" but Callie interrupted him.

"I love you, Dom. Tomorrow can be about talking. Tonight, I just want you to hold me, kiss me, and make love to me. Tonight is about second chances, a celebration of overcoming the past and holding onto each other. Tonight is too precious to waste on thoughts of yesterday or tomorrow."

"I love you too, Darlin'. Tonight is for us."

There was that beautiful word she'd missed hearing from him. They embraced and without a single word between them, they began to sway to the music and stare into each other's eyes. At the end of the song, Dom took Callie by the hand and led her up the stairs to the deck.

"Where is everybody?" asked Callie.

"I booked the place for the night. I wanted you all to myself, but I wanted it to be here."

"You did what? Oh, wait. I remember you. You're the man with the plan."

"That's right, and this is just the beginning."

The sun was slowly sinking into the horizon, and they sat down at the table where they'd shared the first sunset. Things had come full circle, but they certainly had taken the long way to get there. The sunset was even more beautiful than Callie remembered, but perhaps that was because there was so much more love in her heart now.

Dom pulled out all the stops to show Callie how much she meant to him. He'd brought over steak from the ranch and had Gulf shrimp shipped in, a gourmet chocolate cake from a specialty bakery in Germany, along with French champagne. After dinner, Callie was ready for some real alone time with her cowboy, but she couldn't bear any more separation, so they took Dom's car to the ranch, and Dom arranged for one of his ranch hands to pick up Callie's car.

The long weeks of separation from each other made things feel somewhat awkward as they entered the front door of the ranch. They both decided that a dip in the pool and a little more time would rekindle the embers of the fire. Swimming, talking, kissing, embracing their way through the rest of the evening was exactly what Callie and Dom needed to walk into the bedroom and reclaim their relationship completely.

Lying in Dom's arms afterwards, Callie felt blissful and at peace, feelings she wasn't sure would return just 24 hours ago. He whispered in her ear, "I missed you, Darlin', to which she replied, "I missed us." A few minutes later, they were both asleep. The hours and weeks of uncertainty and struggling to remain strong for each other had left them both mentally exhausted, but now there was time to rest.

Callie got up before Dom the next morning and quietly slid out of bed to make him breakfast. Last night had been about her. This morning would be about him. He deserved to be pampered, but she knew she'd have to make it quick if she was going to jump on him in the pampering department. She made French toast, bacon, eggs, hash browns and super strong coffee. She was going to bring a tray to the bed, but the aroma from the coffee called him into the kitchen before she could get it ready.

"Good morning, Cowboy," Callie said with a bright smile.

"Good morning, Sunshine. How did you sleep, and how did you beat me out of bed?"

"I slept like a rock," replied Callie, only smiling at the second question. "What about you?"

Incredulity

"But the most beautiful rock I've ever seen," Dom said with a wink. "I slept like a log. Thank you for breakfast. I'm starving, and this is the best thing I've seen in a few months."

"You're welcome. Watching you eat makes me smile," Callie said, sitting down next to Dom.

Dom cleaned his plate and went for seconds, and Callie poured him another cup of coffee. Dom asked if she could stay the weekend, and of course, no one would be able to drag her away from him for at least another few days. They needed to talk, but she wanted Dom to start the conversation.

"You want to head into town for some lunch later?" asked Dom.

"Sure," Callie responded.

"Awesome. Last one in the shower has to pay," Dom said as he jumped up to run. Callie remembered the shortcut through the guestroom and beat him to the bathroom door. The shower was refreshing, and the next few hours were spent rekindling the fire they'd ignited the night before.

At about 11:30, they got in the car and took off for town. Callie was unsure where they were going, but as long as they were going together, she didn't care. They pulled into the parking lot of a mom-and-pop cafe in Lakeway, and Dom got out to open the door for Callie.

As they walked toward the front door, Dom said, "I invited

someone to join us for lunch, but they may not be here yet. Let's grab a table."

No one had ever been along during any of their time before, and Callie was caught a little off guard. With a puzzled look, she said, "Okay? Who's coming?"

Before Dom could answer, a familiar woman walked up to the table and said, "Hello, Callie. It's great to see you again."

It was June Brett, Brandon's wife. Callie was clueless why June would be having lunch with them. It seemed really strange, since she knew Dom was investigating June's husband and he was now sitting in jail. June reached her hand out to Dom and simply said, "Thank you for everything," leaving Callie even more confused.

Callie simply asked, "Anybody want to fill me in about what we're doing here?"

Dom pulled out Callie's chair, then June's, pulling his chair close to Callie, and began to tell the story of the investigation, Dom's arrest, and the reason June was sitting at the table with them. Dom left his job with the federal government and came back to run the ranch because his dad had died. That part was Dom's real life. Shortly after he moved back, he was contacted by the DEA and brought in on special assignment to investigate Cobra.

Callie listened intently as question after question was

Incredulity

being answered. Dom was then introduced by a CI to Brandon, and about a week into the investigation Dom identified Brandon as the rogue detective within Cobra. Dom made himself invaluable to Brandon by doing most of the risky work, and Brandon was so cocky that the investigation quickly grew against him.

It was about that time that Dom met Callie, so he took extra precautions to be sure no one knew about her and that she wasn't put in harm's way by knowing about them or the investigation. He'd rented an apartment in Austin and put the video camera in the truck. This was simply standard operating procedure for his previous work, and he was really good at it.

He'd met June through dinner at Brandon's and began to socialize with them more often. One night at dinner, Dom noticed bruising around June's neck as she pulled her hair back to do the dishes. When he asked her about it, she said it was nothing. When he pushed her on it, she asked him to leave it alone. Of course, having been in law enforcement for many years, he knew the signs of spousal abuse. He offered her a way out, without risking her life and without having to report it to the police officers she no longer trusted.

As the evidence mounted exponentially against Brandon, Dom became concerned for June's safety, and he told her about the evidence he had and gave her three mailbox keys for safekeeping. He said that if things went south and something happened to him, that she was to anonymously give the mailbox keys to Callie; that she was the only person he trusted to know what to do with the evidence. Dom had told his lawyer about his federal undercover work, but because he had no idea Brandon had taken his truck the night of the murder, he didn't see the relevance in mentioning the hidden camera.

Everything was crystal clear now to Callie. As the three of them sat there around that table, a bond was formed like no other. Callie, Dom and June had worked together to bring down a corrupt detective, an abusive monster, a sadistic murderer. June could move on with her life without fear, and Dom and Callie could enjoy every sunset from this day forward.

June hugged both Dom and Callie and said an early goodbye. She was moving with her children to Dallas and had to get back to packing. Callie reached over and gave Dom a kiss and said, "If ever I doubted your love for me, I am sorry."

Dom took her hand and held it to his face and said, "I take responsibility for placing that doubt there, Darlin'. Can you find it in your heart to forgive me?"

"Already done, Cowboy."

Over the next few weeks, Callie and Dom began to make more time together, more love, more memories. They put on a huge Cowboy Thanksgiving and invited both of their families to

Incredulity

the ranch. As Callie watched the grandkids play and Dom chase around after them, she couldn't help but look up at the sky and whisper, "Thank you, God, for blessing me with this much love."

The first week of December, after weeks of amazing normalcy with Dom, Callie went back to work. It seemed like forever since she'd touched her machine, but she was ready. Things were finally not crazy in her life. She opened her office door early Monday morning to find a white envelope on the floor.

"Are you kidding me?" Callie said, exasperated. "I'm so over the white envelopes. If we have to do this anonymous thing under the door, could we at least make it something other than white?"

She opened the envelope, thinking it had to be a prank. But it wasn't. It was another note from Special Agent Kendrick. As a matter of fact, it was identical to the first note, with a request for a meeting at the same location in 15 minutes. What did he want now? She was done with him. But her curiosity got the best of her, as usual, and she had plenty of time to get there, find out what he wanted and get back to work.

Callie pulled up into the same clandestine parking spot and rolled down her window. "Hello, Callie," said Agent Kendrick. "Thank you for meeting me. I hope you're doing well."

"I'm recovering nicely from the havoc you wreaked on my life," Callie responded. "I'm not dating any of your other agents,

Kathy Zebert

so..."

"I understand your frustration, Callie, but I wanted to see you because the Department of Justice was impressed with the way you handled yourself in Dom's case, and we'd like to fly you to D.C. to talk to us about an analyst's position within the department. We could use someone with your special skills and ethical standards. It wouldn't be anything risky, but it comes with your own private office and it's based out of Austin. What do you think?"

Callie was floored. Did the moon suddenly crash into the sun? She let him know she'd give it some thought and get back to him. This was all too much to decide at 7:30 on a Monday morning, and she'd need to talk to Dom first. They'd agreed there would be no more secrets, and life for them was just getting back to normal.

Agent Kendrick said that would be fine, and Callie drove back to work. She wanted to sit in her spot again and feel like a part of a team. This had been her home for so many years. She couldn't imagine giving it up.

After work, she drove out to the ranch and talked to Dom about the shocking morning meeting with his handler. He was quite surprised and told her that whatever she wanted to do was fine by him. As the afternoon turned into evening and Callie and Dom lay in bed, their bodies intertwined, she looked up at his

Incredulity

gorgeous, sweet face and began to think about the agent's offer.

Would she be happy somewhere else? Was it time for a change in careers? Should she stay where she was, with her wonderful court family? And then she remembered yet another piece of advice from her dad. "If it's not a decision you have to make today, worry about that tomorrow." Besides, those are only two options. Perhaps she'd become a rancher's wife and write a book about her experience.

And with that sweet thought, she held Dom a little closer, kissed him on the cheek and closed her eyes. Life was good.

Made in the USA
Charleston, SC
08 October 2015